Step-Chain

All over the country children go to stay with step-parents, stepbrothers and stepsisters on the weekends. It's just like an endless chain. A step-chain. Y*our Can't Fall For Your Stepsister* is the second link in this step-chain.

I'm Ollie. My parents split up a while ago, and my brother and I live with Mom and Peter, my step-dad. He's more laid back than my real dad, so going on a holiday with him should be fun. Except that Peter's daughters are coming along, too. Girls! I just know there'll be trouble . . .

Collect the links in the step-chain! You never know who you'll meet on the way . . .

Step-Chain

YOU CAN'T FALL FOR YOUR STEP-SISTER

Ann Bryant

Lobster Press™

You Can't Fall For Your Stepsister
© 2001 Series conceived and created by Ann Bryant
© 2001 Cover illustration by Mark Oliver

Published in Canada by:
Lobster Press™
1620 Sherbrooke Street West, Suites C & D
Montréal, Québec   H3H 1C9
Tel. (514) 904-1100 • Fax (514) 904-1101 • www.lobsterpress.com

Publisher: Alison Fripp
Graphic Production: Tammy Desnoyers

Distributed in the United States by:
Publishers Group West
1700 Fourth Street
Berkeley, CA 94710
1-800-788-3123

First published in Great Britain in 2001 by Mammoth,
an imprint of Egmont Children's Books Limited, London

National Library of Canada Cataloguing in Publication

Bryant, Ann
        You can't fall for your stepsister / Ann Bryant.

(Step-chain series ; v. 2)
ISBN 1-894222-77-6

        I. Title. II. Series.

PZ7.B873Yo 2003   j823'.92   C2003-902308-7

Printed and bound in Canada.

CONTENTS

Step-Chain

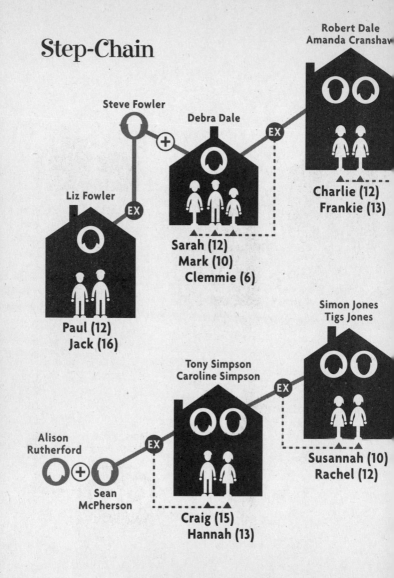

Robert Dale
Amanda Cranshaw

Steve Fowler

Debra Dale

EX

Charlie (12)
Frankie (13)

Liz Fowler

EX

Sarah (12)
Mark (10)
Clemmie (6)

Paul (12)
Jack (16)

Simon Jones
Tigs Jones

Tony Simpson
Caroline Simpson

EX

Susannah (10)
Rachel (12)

Alison
Rutherford

EX

Sean
McPherson

Craig (15)
Hannah (13)

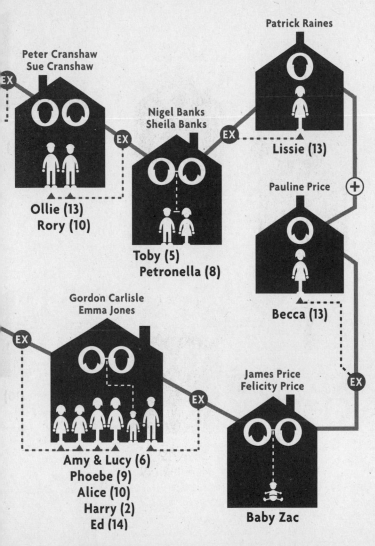

Patrick Raines

Peter Cranshaw
Sue Cranshaw

EX

Nigel Banks
Sheila Banks

EX

Lissie (13)

EX

**Ollie (13)
Rory (10)**

**Toby (5)
Petronella (8)**

Pauline Price

+

Gordon Carlisle
Emma Jones

EX

Becca (13)

James Price
Felicity Price

EX

**Amy & Lucy (6)
Phoebe (9)
Alice (10)
Harry (2)
Ed (14)**

Baby Zac

Read on to discover all the links . . .

1. THE COUNTDOWN

My name's Oliver Banks. That's the longest version, strictly reserved for teachers – *"Oliver Banks, I don't appear to have received your homework."* Then there's Oliver, which is what Mom calls me when she's not happy. But my friends all call me Ollie.

I live with my mom and my stepdad, Peter. He's really cool. He jokes around a lot and isn't as strict as my real dad. Not that I like my real dad any less than Peter. It's just that he's not so laid back.

Right now it's summer vacation and I'm counting down the days till we go away for a couple weeks in New Jersey. Only three to go. I *think* I'm looking forward to it, but I'm not totally sure. The people going from my family are me, my mom, Peter and my brother Rory.

Fine so far. But . . . get this! Peter wants to bring his two daughters along. They don't live with us. They live with their mom, but come here to visit their dad (Peter) quite often. They're called Frankie and Charlie. I'm usually at my dad's when they come here, so I don't really get to see them all that much. Once or twice Charlie's been here on her own, and she seems OK, mucking about with Rory in the backyard or on his precious computer.

But going on holiday together – that's different. I bet Frankie and Charlie don't want to go away with two boys, any more than I want to go away with two girls.

"Oliver?"

Uh-oh! Mom didn't sound too happy.

"Yeah?" I answered, opening my bedroom door.

"How many times have I got to tell you to take your sneakers off at the back door?" she called up the stairs.

"But I came in at the front. With Peter."

"I realize that. There's a trail of muddy footprints going through the hall and all the way upstairs. I presume they go right into your bedroom. Come to the top of the stairs. Let me look at you."

I quickly took the sneakers off without undoing the laces, then went to the top of the stairs.

"Oh, Ollie. What am I going to do with you?"

"What's wrong? I've taken my trainers off."

"But your trackpants and your shirt are absolutely filthy! Do your friends go home looking as though they've been having a mud bath?"

Mom was exaggerating and she knew it. "You can't help getting dirty if you're playing football, Mom. Peter didn't tell me off," I couldn't resist adding.

"Peter probably didn't even notice. Anyway, I'm not arguing about it. Go and have a bath and by the time you've done that, dinner will be ready."

And that was when I remembered that I was supposed to be taking a video back to Sam Cotteril's. I'd promised I'd definitely do it today, because it belongs to his much older brother, who's going ape because I keep forgetting to give it back.

The trouble was, knowing Mom, there was no chance she'd let me go to Sam's even if I got down on my bended knee and begged. So there was only one thing to do.

I ran the bath water at top force, then turned the taps off, shut the bathroom door, and snuck downstairs and out the front door with the video. I got to Sam's in a record seven minutes.

"Hiya, Ollie. You look winded," he said, opening the door. "You can't be very fit. You should get yourself in training."

He grinned because everyone knows that Sam is the least fit person in the universe.

"Cut out the chat, Sam. I'm supposed to be in the bath. I'm risking another big blow-up from Mom, bringing this back for you."

"Bet you'd like to have a quick go on my new computer game though," he said, grinning even more and opening the door wider. "It only takes a few minutes and it's awesome, I can tell you."

I knew I should have just said no. Sam must have seen the hesitation on my face. (He could hardly have missed it — I was biting my lip and screwing my eyes up trying not to give in to temptation.)

"The thing is, Ollie," said Sam, yanking me in through the front door, "if you go home right away your body won't have had time to recover, but if you just rest for a few minutes you'll get back much faster, honest."

It seemed to make sense.

"OK. Only a few minutes though."

Sam's mom called out when Sam and I were practically at the top of the stairs. She's scary, Sam's mom. Her voice sounds too loud for the room. You're not supposed to use the word fat, so let's just say she's quite large and she always wears big swirly dresses, in bright colors like orange. Her hair's weird too. Sort of speckled blondish gray and shiny.

"Is that Oliver Banks, by any chance?" she boomed up the stairs. I turned around and gave her a shaky smile.

"Hello, Mrs. Cotteril." I've never had the guts to call her Pammy, which is what she likes people to call her. It just sounds stupid.

"I'm glad you're here, Oliver, because Samson – " I tried not to smirk " – tells me that your family is off to New Jersey in a few days' time, too. Such a coincidence!"

The bangles on her arm started jangling, like she needed a fanfare to go with her loud voice. I made a noise that was supposed to show that I agreed about the coincidence but didn't really want to talk about it any more.

"Ollie's only got a minute, Mom," said Sam, going up the last two stairs. I was about to follow when . . .

"Are you going anywhere near Ashbury Park on your travels, by any chance, Oliver?" Mrs. C's big voice rang up the stairwell.

"Um . . . I'm not sure – "

"What's the name of the place where you're staying? Hmm?"

"Um . . . Atlantic City."

She clapped her hands together and the clap echoed all the way up the stairs.

"Incredible! Such a coincidence! It's scarcely a stone's throw from Ashbury Park. Marvelous news. I will telephone your mother straight away and arrange a little get-together. We're staying with my sister and her daughter. Samson wasn't too sure that he wanted to spend a week in all-female company, were you, Samson?"

I whacked Sam's leg as subtly as I could to get him to stop his mom from phoning my mom. That would be just great, wouldn't it, when I was supposed to be in the bath? Sam must have thought I was trying to get away so we could play the computer game, because he turned and headed for his bedroom. His mom was still banging on in her foghorn voice, "But now you know Oliver is going to be around, I think we might detect a bit of an improvement in your attitude, hmm?"

"Um . . . actually, Mrs. Cotteril, Mom's out at the moment. I'll tell her to call you when she gets back."

"All right, Oliver. Thank you, dear."

And she went off singing in a high warbly voice in a foreign language. Poor Sam! I was glad my mom was quite an ordinary sort of mother so my friends couldn't make fun of me. It'd be good if he was near us on holiday though. But something told me Mom wasn't going to be too pleased. I don't think she's ever liked Mrs. Cotteril all that much.

It was beginning to look like coming to Sam's was one big mistake.

2. PETER THE PEACEMAKER

It was twenty-three minutes later when I got home. I'd got a key for the front door but I knew it'd make a noise when I opened it, so I reckoned the back would be safer. The only problem was getting through the kitchen without Mom seeing me. I peered in through the window and saw that the coast was clear. The windows were pretty steamed up though, which meant that dinner must be nearly ready, so Mom would be back in the kitchen at any minute.

The back door hardly made a sound as I opened it. I just had to get upstairs without being seen. I took off my sneakers and tiptoed, quiet as a cat burglar, through the kitchen and the hall, then up the stairs. (Rory was in his bedroom. I could hear racing car noises coming from his computer.) I crept into the bathroom, took all my clothes off, sat in the bath for about five seconds, ripped the icicles off me, got straight out again, rubbed myself dry, then went back to my room to find some clean clothes. I couldn't help smiling to myself as I got dressed. It was so easy to fool Mom.

"Shall I put these dirty jeans in the washing machine?" I asked her, trying not to sound *too* smug, as I went into the kitchen a few minutes later.

I could only just make her out in the middle of the steam from all the pans. She was straining the peas. Perfect timing, Ollie!

"Yes, that's what we normally do with dirty clothes," she replied. I didn't like that sarcastic tone. It meant she was still mad. Dunno why — I'd had a bath (or so she thought) and I'd even brought my jeans down for the wash. "Put the plates on the table then go and tell Rory and Peter that it's ready, will you?"

The four of us were digging into this cheesy pasta stuff, when all became clear.

"Frankie phoned," Rory said.

He had a sort of lopsided grin on his face. This was the expression my sly little brother always wore when he was trying to get me into trouble. I'd thought he was talking to Mom, but everyone was staring at me. Uh-oh! About to be busted, Ollie!

"Yeah?" I said, flashing my innocent look round the table, even though I could see what was coming a mile off.

"She wanted to speak to you," Mom told me,

raising her eyebrows slightly.

"So . . . did you say I was in the bath?" Keep cool.

"I knocked on the bathroom door to find out how long you were going to be," Mom carried on, in her steely *I-am-going-to-kill-you* voice.

One look at her face (which matched the voice) and I knew she'd got me. Quick change of tactic needed here.

"It wasn't my fault, Mom. I had to take this video back to Sam's brother. I promised I would."

"It's a shame you didn't ask."

"You would have said I wasn't allowed."

I noticed Peter was keeping his head really close to his food, probably so no one would see that he was grinning.

"That's not the point. Sneaking off like that is exactly the same as lying."

"Sorry," I mumbled. "Anyway, what did Frankie want?"

It was a smart move asking that question because one: it would get us off the subject of me and the phantom bath, and two: it might give me a clue about Frankie. I needed all the clues I could get. I mean, I wasn't about to go around broadcasting it, but the thought of this holiday with two girls was scaring me to death. Charlie, the twelve-year-old, seemed all right — a bit bossy and far too chatty — but basically pretty normal. It was Frankie, the thirteener, I was worried about.

"She was actually calling to speak to *me*. She wanted to find out whether she'd need to take any fancier clothes on holiday," said Mom.

Fancy clothes? On a holiday? Give me a break!

"What did you tell her?"

"I said it might be an idea to take one nice pair of pants or a skirt, just in case."

"In case of what? You're not planning on taking us to any boring concerts, I hope!"

"We haven't planned anything, but if you play much more football in the next few days, you won't be taking any clothes at all because they'll all be in the wash."

"That'd be good," Rory giggled. "Ollie in the nude. Bet Frankie'd love that."

I rolled my eyes at the ceiling, pretending I thought Rory was stupid, but actually, he'd got me worried. I started imagining how awful it would be if Frankie suddenly came in to the bathroom and caught me butt-naked.

"Don't be silly," said Mom.

And my stepdad Peter did the same look as I'd just done, to show that he agreed with me. He's great, Peter. He never really gets angry with me. When Mom tells me off he doesn't interfere. He just sits there quietly, and then finds a way to take her mind off the subject.

"So what did Frankie want to speak to *me* for?" I asked, looking out of the window as though I wasn't that interested really.

"She didn't say. She just asked if she could have a quick word with you."

"Maybe she wanted to know if you were taking any make-up, Ollie," giggled Rory.

"Excuse me while I die laughing," I said, giving Rory my hardest look. But he'd got me imagining stuff again. I didn't like the thought of girly things like make-up all over the place.

"She'd better not be taking make-up," I said, "otherwise it'll take ten times longer to get ready to go out anywhere."

"Don't exaggerate, Ollie," said Mom. "And stop complaining. It works both ways. Boys can be very irritating to girls too, you know."

"What about clearing the table?" Peter suddenly changed the subject. "It'll be good practice for when we're on holiday."

And with that he leapt up and started rushing around, grabbing everyone's plates.

"Quite right. Up you go," said Mom. "When we're away, you boys must make sure you do at least as much helping as the girls."

Mom's remark must have slipped into my subconscious because that night I dreamt that Frankie and Charlie were reclining on golden benches, wearing long flowing orange dresses and painting their toenails, while Peter, Rory and I waited on them hand and foot.

It was a nightmare, I can tell you.

3. GIRL POWER!
(THAT'S WHAT *THEY* THINK)

"Peter'll be back with Charlie and Frankie in about five minutes, you two," Mom called up the stairs. "Bring your bags down so we can load the car and set off right away."

"Can I have your cell phone for the trip, Mom?" I called down to her.

"Whatever for?"

"I want to play that Snakes game on it."

"Well, I don't mind you playing the odd game on it, but I don't want you ignoring Frankie, Ollie."

"I'm not her personal entertainer, am I? I notice you don't tell Rory not to ignore Charlie."

"Charlie's got a set of travel games for two people to play. She and Rory have been talking on the phone about it. I just don't want poor Frankie to be left out, that's all."

Great! I thought. The holiday hasn't even started, and already Frankie's spoiling it.

As I was thinking that, I glanced through the hall window and saw the car backing into the drive. Frankie and Charlie were looking out of the rear window. I quickly ducked before they saw me.

It was a boiling hot day and it felt really stuffy in the car, but Peter had recently bought a minivan, so at least we weren't squashed. I'd arranged it so Charlie, Rory and Frankie sat together in the middle row and I sat behind them in the back. That meant I didn't have to talk to anyone, because it's really difficult to hear what people are saying when you're so far back.

I couldn't stop staring at Frankie and Charlie's long blonde hair. They looked pretty much identical from behind. Frankie was right in front of me. I'd never seen their hair at such close quarters before. It looked like dolls' hair, kind of shiny and wiry, and I kept getting this urge to touch Frankie's. At one point, when the others were deep into Travel Scrabble and Frankie was staring out of the window, I reached out to touch the ends, but at that very moment she suddenly swung round and asked me if I wanted to play twenty questions. I shook my head and pretended I was reading my comic book, and luckily she turned around again pretty quickly, so I don't think she saw my red face.

We stopped in a picnic area at twelve o'clock. Everyone except Rory got out of the car to eat their sandwiches and chips and stuff. Rory hardly ate a thing. He'd found my Game Boy and wanted as many turns on it as possible before we set off again.

"Come on, Rory," said Peter after a while. "Get out and stretch your legs."

Rory took him literally and got Frankie to hold him under the arms while Charlie pulled his feet. He thought it was such a witty thing to do, poor, pathetic boy! It was the kind of thing Sam would have done. Which reminded me . . .

"Mom, did Mrs. Cotteril phone you?"

"Yes," said Mom, rolling her eyes. "She wants us to meet up one day."

"Who's Mrs. Cotteril?" asked Charlie.

"She's Ollie's friend's mom."

"Does that mean we're meeting your friend as well, Ollie?" asked Frankie.

"Dunno."

"Yes, we are," Mom told Frankie, giving me

a look that said, *Don't be so rude*.

"Oh great! What's his name?"

"Sam."

"Has he got any brothers or sisters?" asked Charlie.

"One," I told her.

"Sam's brother, Gareth, is twenty-one," Mom explained, giving me another of her hard looks, "so he's not going to New Jersey. But apparently Sam and his mom are staying with Sam's auntie Letitia and her daughter, Daisy."

"How old's Daisy?" asked Charlie.

"I think she's about your age."

Oh, great!

When we got back in the car, Mom and Peter swapped places. Peter joked that Mom had to drive the last part because he didn't want her navigating when we got near to the place where we were staying.

"You know what your mom's like, boys. We

don't want to wind up in Maine, do we?"

"Peter, on the other hand, has got the most perfect map-reading skills," Mom said. She was smiling. I *think* it was a joke.

The funny thing was that when we were within a few miles of the place, Peter's great skills went wrong and we got totally lost.

"You're hopeless, Dad," said Frankie. "Here, give me the map and the instructions."

She read the instructions in about ten seconds and then studied the map for less than half a minute.

"Oh, I see where we've gone wrong. OK, Sue, take the next left and that should bring us out parallel with the road we took off the express way."

I was astonished by the way she'd figured it out so easily. She then proceeded to give Mom directions for the next five minutes. And what do you know, we were there!

"Wow, Frankie! Well done!" said Mom as she pulled up outside the house that was to be ours for the next two weeks. "Girl power!"

I laughed. We all did because it sounded so weird hearing Mom use that expression.

"It's not very big," said Rory, eyeing the house.

"I did warn you," said Mom.

"It looks really sweet," said Charlie. "Quaint and cozy."

And then a woman appeared from next door.

"Hello! You're early!" she said. "You're lucky though. The last bunch left at the crack of dawn, so it's all clean and ready for you."

Mom thanked her and took the key.

"It's going to be great," said Peter. "The sun's shining, the birds are singing. We're five minutes from the beach. What more could we want?'

"Let's get going then," I said.

"We've got to unpack first," said Charlie.

"Yeah, let's do it as fast as we can and then go straight to the beach," said Rory.

Huh! Fat chance of that happening with girls around.

"Peter and I have been driving for the last five and a half hours, you two. We don't really want to get in the car again straight away," said Mom.

"I'll make you a nice cup of tea," said Frankie, sucking up to Mom.

"What a lovely idea," said Mom, giving Frankie her biggest smile.

I knew this would happen. The girls were taking Mom's side right from the start. We three wouldn't stand a chance. The only good thing was that Charlie was very fast at taking her bags in. The moment she'd dumped them in the hall she went charging around the house calling out to the rest of us what every single room looked like before we got to it ourselves.

"The kitchen's pretty and big — microwave

and everything . . . the living-room's quite big too . . . TV's a bit small, but really comfy couches . . . Oh, can this be Frankie's and my bedroom? You can actually see the ocean out of this window. Oh, double bed . . . right . . . Well, we'll have this room then. It's got pink in it, Rory. You'd hate it . . . The bathroom's nice . . . Oh no! There's only one bathroom! No, wait a minute, there's a separate toilet here . . . And this bedroom'll be best for Ollie and Rory. The closet's bigger than ours, but I don't like the carpet very much."

"Got it sorted out then?" Peter asked Charlie as he dumped his and Mom's suitcases on the double bed. "How about seeing if the boys have got any views on the subject?"

"This bedroom will be OK for us two, won't it, Rory?" I said quickly.

I needn't have bothered to ask. Rory didn't care. He was already pulling clothes out of his bag and chucking them on the bed, in the room that Charlie wanted us to have.

"Hurry up, you two," he called out to Mom and Peter. "The sooner you sit down, the sooner the hour will be over."

Mom laughed as she came upstairs. "I didn't mean exactly an hour, Rory. I just don't want to hurry, that's all." She poked her head round our door. "And fold those clothes neatly and put them in the drawer."

By the time Mom and Peter came downstairs, Frankie had unpacked everything that we'd brought for the kitchen and she'd even made snacks and set them out on the table.

"How nice! I can tell this is going to be a wonderful holiday!" said Mom, smiling at Frankie and Charlie.

For *her* maybe. Not for me.

4. THE BIGGEST WAVE

At about three-thirty we packed all the beach things and set off. The roads were very narrow and winding so we had to go slowly. It seemed to take ages and I was boiling hot. I couldn't wait to go in the ocean.

"It's busy, isn't it?" said Mom, looking at the crowded beach.

"Never mind, we'll find a little spot some-where, I'm sure," said Peter.

Just then a whole family started to pack up their things about five yards away, so I ran on ahead and grabbed their place.

"This is perfect," said Mom, smiling around happily as she slapped sun block on her legs a few minutes later. Charlie sat down next to her and did exactly the same thing. So far it was going just as I wanted. Mom and the girls would sunbathe while Rory, Peter and I would body-board and stuff.

I glanced over at Frankie. She had her back to the rest of us and was pulling the top half of her swimsuit up. I quickly pretended to be looking at something in the sand because I didn't want Rory piping up, *Ollie's staring at Frankie getting changed, Mom!* which was the kind of thing the little toerag would say just to tick me off. I did have another glance though.

"Come on, Peter, let's go and surf," I said.

"Bit cold for me, Ollie," said Peter, sitting down on the other side of Mom.

"Cold? It's boiling!"

"It might be boiling to you, Ollie, but we delicate grown-up people feel the cold more than you do," joked Mom.

"Come on, Rory," I said. But he was fishing around in one of the big plastic bags full of beach stuff.

"Where's the bucket and shovel, Mom?" he asked, sounding frantic.

"Don't worry," said Mom, "it's in the other bag."

"Aren't you coming into the water?" I asked him.

"Nope. I'm going to build a castle with a moat around it. You can help if you want. Did you pack two shovels, Mom?"

"I packed four actually," said Mom.

I suddenly wished I was like Rory – a ten-year-old boy who didn't give a microchip about anything. And that's when the first shock of the day happened.

"I'll go into the water with you, Ollie," said

Frankie, fishing in one of the bags for something.

"Um . . . don't you want to sunbathe?" I asked her, praying that she'd say yes and stay with the others. I didn't want her coming in the water with me. It wouldn't be the same. I mean, she was a girl! Well, more like a sister, I suppose. But then I didn't really know her properly. I wouldn't be able to muck about with her — not like I do with Rory or Sam.

"No, I want to go in the water. Honestly," she said, twisting her hair up on to the top of her head. This time it was impossible not to stare. I couldn't figure out how she was going to squash so much hair into one little hairband thing, but somehow it worked.

"Are you sure you're not just being kind to Ollie?" Mom asked her.

"No, I love the ocean," she answered.

Now what was I going to do? I looked at the

water. The tide was pretty far out, which meant that it would take ages to get there. If it was Rory and me we'd run fast all the way, and splash each other in the rock pools. No way was I about to do that with Frankie! You never know with girls. She might go moaning back to Peter that I'd wet her hair or something.

"Come on. Race you!" Frankie grabbed one of the body boards and set off running. She left me standing there looking like a complete dork with my mouth hanging open.

Two boys who were probably a couple of years older than me walked past at that moment. They looked at Frankie then nudged each other and grinned. They must have thought she looked nice. I wondered if they thought she was my sister or my girlfriend or what. I suddenly realized I was still standing there, and Frankie was getting a bit too much of a start. Never mind, it wouldn't take long to catch up to her.

Just as I was setting off with the other body board, she stopped.

"Keep going. I'll catch up!" I called out.

But she just stood there waiting for me to work my way around all the people on the beach. When I drew level with her she broke into a run.

"I didn't want to have an unfair advantage," she laughed.

Right, Frankie, if you want a race, you can have a race!

I put on a big spurt and overtook her almost immediately. Neither of us spoke for a while, but I knew she wasn't far behind because I could hear her pounding footsteps. After a minute the sweat was pouring down my back and my arm ached because the body board was so light that the wind kept forcing it sideways. I wished I could turn around to see how Frankie was coping with her board, but that would lose me

time. I looked at the ocean in the distance —
there was still quite a way to go.

"Want to stop, Ollie?"

"What for?"

"I just wondered if you thought it was too hot
for running."

"No. You can, if you want."

"No, I'm OK."

Pity!

So on we ran, my legs feeling heavier and
heavier with every footstep. I couldn't help
slackening the pace a bit, and thank goodness,
she did the same, so after another minute we
were jogging along side by side. I hoped she'd
forgotten it was a race. I hoped in vain, because as
soon as we came to within a couple yards of the
water, she suddenly put on a big spurt, kicking
and splashing her way in, while I followed, trying
to keep up. Then she chucked the body board to
one side and dove under a wave.

"Think that makes me the winner," she said a moment later, throwing her arms up to the sky and falling back into the ocean, laughing. She was still laughing when she came up the second time. "This is so amazing, Ollie, isn't it?"

I didn't answer, just started looking for a really big wave. As she'd won the race, I wanted to make sure that at least I out-surfed her, otherwise she'd think I was a total nerd.

My luck was in. An enormous wave was gathering up right behind me. I'd body-surfed lots of times on holiday last year. You have to judge exactly the right moment to plunge forward on to the board. I knew this was going to be a good one and I was right. It was perfect. The feeling you get when the wave scoops you up and sweeps you along is really great. It took me right to the shore.

"That was awesome, Ollie!" called Frankie. "My turn now."

She didn't choose such a powerful wave as the one I'd chosen and she took off just a moment too soon, but still managed to come quite far.

"You're better at it than me. I plunged in too soon," she said as she drew level with me. "Let's try again. It's great!"

But I was standing there with my mouth hanging open again, wasn't I? I just didn't get it. None of my friends would ever admit that I was better than them at anything – not even Sam. (And I suppose if I've got a best friend, it must be him, even though we don't have that much in common. He's pretty useless at sports but really good at everything else, and he's a great laugh.) So was it a girl thing, or was it just a Frankie thing?

We surfed for at least half an hour and it was the most fun I'd had in ages. Frankie got quite good at it and said we should try racing. I won nearly all the races but she didn't seem to mind.

On one race the wave shot my board right into her shoulder. She made a sort of gasping noise and I thought it must have really hurt her. She stood up and rubbed her arm, but I couldn't see her face because her hair had all fallen out of the thing on top of her head.

"Are you OK?"

"Yeah . . . thanks."

I was amazed. I expected her to storm off in a big huff but nothing else happened. Then Rory and Charlie appeared.

"Hi, you two. Can we have the boards for a while?" Charlie said.

It was only fair that we handed them over, but I felt a bit kind of lost with nothing to do except splash about. It would have been all right with Peter or Rory or one of my friends, but I wasn't sure what to do with Frankie. Last year on holiday Rory was always jumping on me, then he had to try and hang on while I used all my strength to try and chuck him off. It worked the other way around too, because of the water making you lighter. There was no way I could play that with Frankie because our bodies'd have to touch and that would have been far too embarrassing.

"I'll go back and get a ball and we can chuck it around in the water," Frankie suggested. "OK?"

I couldn't believe my luck. She wanted to do all the things I thought she'd hate. It might be an idea if I got the ball myself though. If she told Mom or Peter about her shoulder, they'd try to get her to sit down for a while, and I'd have no one to hang out with. It was so odd that I was thinking like this. I never thought I'd find it so much fun being with Frankie.

"I'll go," I said.

But I was too late. She was already leaping through the waves, her knees and feet sticking out and kicking at odd angles. She really didn't care. I never knew girls acted like this.

Rory and Charlie were trying to stand on the body boards. They were laughing hysterically because they kept falling off. As Frankie passed them they called out to her, so she didn't notice those same two boys that I'd spotted looking at her earlier, running past. They both whistled loudly as she broke into a jog. She must have heard them, but she didn't turn around or anything. They stared at her for a while, then splashed their way into the ocean. Something tightened inside me. I wasn't sure why, but I wished they hadn't whistled.

And that was when it hit me. Just like being knocked over by the biggest wave in the ocean. I was jealous of those boys! I didn't want them looking at Frankie like that.

But then right afterwards there was this massive confusion inside my head because Frankie's my stepsister, and *step*sister is only a step away from *real* sister. Literally! And you don't get jealous because of your real sister, do you? So why was I jealous? I didn't get it. It was really messing with my head, all this step stuff.

5. RORY STARTS STIRRING

I bolted upright in bed. Something was wrong. What was Rory doing fast asleep in my room? Why were there two beds, anyway? I blinked about ten times to try and shake the sleep away, then I took a better look around and realized where I was. Of course! We were on holiday. Great! No school, no work, just beach and . . .

That's when I remembered. Frankie.

I'd been thinking about the jealousy thing right up until bedtime the day before. And when I'd gone to bed, I couldn't get to sleep for ages because I was really worried. If I was jealous of those boys, I must have a thing for Frankie! It was totally gross. You can't fall for your own stepsister. She was practically my sister, for god's sake, so I had to get all those stupid thoughts out of my head once and for all. Trouble was, this was a brand new day and I didn't feel any different. How could I make the thoughts go away? They were stuck there.

I got out of bed and was about to get dressed when I found myself smelling my armpits.

Ollie, you nerd, what are you doing?

I'd only just told myself to get a grip when here I was sniffing my armpits. It was a good thing I did though, because they were a bit funky. I went into the bathroom to see if there was any deodorant. My luck was in. I sprayed it all over me for good measure, then went back to my room to get dressed.

I was just about to put yesterday's clothes on

when I stopped. I might look better in something different.

What! Are you out of your mind, Ollie? It was happening again. Now I was even thinking what Frankie might like me to be wearing. How lame is that! I really had to put a stop to this Frankiemania before it got out of control.

I grabbed yesterday's clothes and put them on. Then I yanked back the curtains to check if it was going to be a good day for the beach.

The light streaming in made Rory grunt, but he didn't wake up completely. I was just about to whiz downstairs when I thought I saw some Morse code flashes through the trees across the road. I looked again and realized it was only the sun glinting. Maybe I'd tell Frankie about it though. In fact if she was awake I could even show her. She'd appreciate that, I know, because yesterday evening she'd made us all go to her bedroom window and look at the sun setting.

"What are you smiling at?" Rory's squeaky morning voice interrupted my thoughts.

"I wasn't smiling."

"Yes, you were. It looked really girly."

I didn't bother to answer, just went downstairs. But I realized at that moment that I'd have to be very careful. My life wouldn't be worth living if Rory ever found out that I'd got a thing for Frankie. You see, Rory makes a point of noticing everything I say and do, then he jumps on the tiniest embarrassing thing and bugs me with it just to tick me off. (He's got this friend called Nick. Nick's got an older brother too, and I think Rory and Nick have got some kind of competition going to see who can get under their brother's skin the most.)

Right now, I need Rory around about as much as I need a broken leg. It feels like I'm under a magnifying glass. I'm going to have to make sure I don't even look at Frankie if Rory's anywhere within fifty feet. It's certainly not going to be a picnic, stuck in this little house.

"Mom, what day are we supposed to be meeting up with Sam and his parents?" I asked at breakfast.

"I'd forgotten about that," replied Mom, her voice going all flat. "I said we'd meet them in Ashbury Park on Thursday."

"Who's Sam again?" asked Charlie.

"Ollie's weird friend," Rory answered.

I didn't want Frankie to think I'd got any weird friends, but on the other hand, it was true. Sam *was* weird.

"There's nothing wrong with weird people," said Frankie.

It sounded like she was sticking up for me, and before I realized it I found I was smiling at her. Big mistake! Rory was wearing one of his lopsided grins so I knew he was about to stir up some trouble. It was a shame I couldn't reach across the table and strangle the life out of him. Strangling was obviously out, but I had to do something quickly. Instead I stretched the smile into a sort of leer, went cross-eyed and wagged my head from side to side, so it looked as though I was making fun of Frankie for trying to be clever. Immediately her face fell and she went pink. I wanted to kick myself and then kick Rory for making me do that.

Frankie, still blushing, got up and took her plate and mug over to the sink.

"Come on, you two," said Mom to Rory and me. "Remember what we said about everyone helping."

I leapt to my feet and made a lunge for the sink because there was a small shred of hope that I might be able to put things right with Frankie, out of earshot of everyone else.

"That's what he does — Sam," I mumbled

when I was right beside her, with our backs to the others.

"What?"

"That face and that wiggling thing. He's always doing that. He's really weird!"

Frankie turned slowly to look at me. I think she was trying to search my expression to see whether or not I was joking. Her face was only about five inches from mine and I could see the freckles on her nose and the way her eyelashes went straight down and didn't curl at all. Everything inside me knotted up and then came back to normal again. That had never happened before. It gave me a shock.

The first I knew that Rory had been creeping up on us was when his face suddenly popped up right between mine and Frankie's.

"Caught you!" he said in a sing-song voice.

"Don't be stupid," I said, knowing that I was a bit pink. "We were just – "

"What? Checking each other for zits?" said Rory, then he nearly fell over, laughing at his witty remark.

I expect the pink turned bright red, but with any luck I managed to hide it by making a dive for the garbage can, whipping out the garbage bag and going to the door.

"Well done, Ollie," said Peter. "The water down here must be doing you good. I've never known you to empty the garbage without being asked."

"It's 'cuz he's getting girly," said Rory.

When I came back Rory decided to carry on with his stupid theme.

"This morning Ollie was smiling out of the window at the view. I mean, that's not normal, is it?"

"It was a really nice sunrise," I mumbled, looking at my feet and feeling totally embarrassed, but desperately wanting Frankie to know that she wasn't the only one to appreciate that kind of thing.

When I looked up, I found that everyone was looking at me in a peculiar way, as though I'd started foaming at the mouth. I must have gone a bit too far with my sunrise remark. I'd have to tone it down a bit in future.

"Let's go to the beach," I changed the subject.

"Yes, we don't want to waste a single second of this glorious weather," said Mom.

Phew! Close one!

6. SPIT!

We spent most of that day and the next two days at the beach. It was really weird because no matter what I was doing – surfing, swimming, playing Frisbee – my mind was on Frankie. I knew it was stupid but I kept imagining she was watching me. So say I was watching TV, I'd have to keep checking I didn't have my mouth hanging open or anything, because if she happened to be looking at that moment, she'd think I was totally uncool. Things like picking your nose or even yawning were definitely out.

Sometimes I got mad at myself for having such pathetic thoughts, and then I'd start wondering what Frankie really thought about me. She probably didn't notice me – and even if she did, she probably couldn't care less what I looked like. But she did act as though she liked me a lot – I mean, much more than Rory. And it was true that she seemed to prefer being with me to being with Charlie. But that didn't mean anything, did it?

On Wednesday the weather broke. When I woke up and looked out of my window to find it all gray, I felt instantly depressed. It looked like the beach was out, which sucked because that was one great place for getting away from Hawkeye Rory, and I'd got used to having Frankie all to myself in the ocean.

"What are we going to do today?" Frankie asked at breakfast time.

"What's wrong with the beach?" I asked as casually as I could, just in case by some miracle the others agreed.

"You're joking!" said Mom. "We'd freeze on the beach."

"Not if you do stuff," I carried on desperately.

"Like what?" asked Peter.

"Play Frisbee or ball or build sandcastles. It'd be a great day for building castles," I told Rory, "because there'd be hardly anyone about, so you could make the biggest sandcastle ever."

And when we get there I'll soon convince Frankie that the ocean feels warmer in the rain.

"Have you actually looked out of the window this morning, Ollie?" Peter asked me with a puzzled sort of grin.

I was just waiting for Rory to come out with some embarrassing comment, when Charlie suddenly said, "I like it when it rains."

"See!" I said, giving Peter a look. "Not everyone's as chicken as you and Mom."

"I wasn't going to say that," said Charlie. "I was going to say, I like it when it rains because we can stay here and be all cozy together."

Yuck! Not likely.

"You don't go on holiday to stay in all day," I told her. "What about Quasar Laser, Mom? Or an arcade?"

"I think it would be a good chance to explore some of these pretty little coastal villages. Don't you, Peter?" said Mom.

"Maybe we should compromise — a bit of exploring and a bit of amusement arcade-type stuff."

"Yeah, or a theme park," I said, trying to get Mom away from her boring sightseeing idea.

"Yeah, a theme park!" said Frankie and Rory at exactly the same time.

And at that very moment there was a flash of lightning and a giant crack of thunder.

Frankie suddenly rushed over to Peter and he put his arm around her. "Frankie's never liked storms," he explained to the rest of us, while she kept her face hidden.

"*I* love them!" said Charlie, rushing to the front door to look at the sky.

I was thinking what a shame the others were all there. If it had just been Frankie and me, *I* would have had to put my arm around her. Not Peter. My stomach did that tightening thing again at the thought of her being that close to me.

"Let's get into teams and have a games tournament while it's raining," said Charlie, "then go out later. We brought quite a few games, didn't we, Sue?"

"Well, we've got two packs of cards and Connect Four," said Mom.

All our names were put in a bowl, then Rory read out the pairs for the teams. It came out that he and I were together, Frankie and Mom were together, and Charlie and Peter.

Just my luck! Let's hope we can get the whole thing over and done with pretty fast, then go out somewhere.

I watched Charlie and Frankie marking out the big score sheet, their heads together as they leaned over the table. I'd seen Rory and Charlie with their heads like that when they'd been digging in the sand, so nobody would think it weird if Frankie and I got that close. If Rory dared to say anything I'd turn to Frankie and say, *Sorry about my little brother. He's going for the Idiot of the Year award*. Yeah, that would be good. She'd find that really witty.

Rory taught us all how to play this mega-fast card game called Spit. Only two people can play at once so whoever wasn't playing, played a quick game of Connect Four. I didn't get to play Frankie at Spit until the very end of the whole tournament.

"If Frankie wins this, her team has won the whole thing, but if Ollie wins, that makes *us* two the winners," Rory said, practically jumping up and down with excitement. "So come on, Ollie!" he added, slapping me on the back.

"Come on, Frankie!" said Mom, getting pretty excited (for her) too.

"Right," said Peter, "this is serious stuff. You'd better shake hands, you two, before you start."

My eyes met Frankie's as our hands touched and I went all kind of dizzy. Something must have shown in my face because Rory suddenly cupped his hand around his mouth and whispered in my ear, "You like Frankie, don't you?"

I felt like whacking him one, but I knew I had to stay cool otherwise he'd know he'd hit the nail on the head, and that would be the pits. So I gave him a *stop being so pathetic* look and started laying out the cards.

"One, two, three, go!" said Mom when we were both ready.

"Come on, Ollie!" Rory screeched in my ear.

I was going much faster than Frankie and I figured I could easily beat her, but I'd feel really sorry for her if she didn't win, because she'd think she was letting Mom down.

"Come on, Frankie!" said Mom.

I glanced at the cards on Frankie's side of the table. She still had loads left to turn over and I'd only got a few. I had to do something drastic or I'd win at any moment. Then poor Frankie would have to suffer Rory crowing about us two being the winners. And then Mom would make it worse by coming out with something diplomatic about how it was only luck anyway, when it was perfectly obvious it was a game of skill.

I couldn't bear it any longer. I deliberately dropped one of my cards on the floor and then spent ages pretending to try and pick it up off the carpet.

"I'll get it, Ollie, you moron," said Rory diving under the table. "You get on with the game. You dropped that card on purpose."

"No, I didn't," I snapped back at him, but my cheeks felt hot.

"Yes, you did," said Rory. "You've gone all red again. That proves it."

Frankie was piling on the cards quite quickly now. Good. I only needed to hang on playing dumb for another few seconds and she'd win.

"It's not fair!" screeched Rory. "He's going slow on purpose." Then he turned to Peter. "This game doesn't count, does it?"

"Out!" cried Frankie, clapping her hands together.

She jumped up and gave Mom a big hug, then they started dancing around together like a pair of schoolgirls. "We won! We won!"

"It wasn't fair," repeated Rory through his black scowl. "Ollie deliberately let her win."

"Don't be silly," said Mom. "It's only a game."

"He's in love with her," Rory went on in his big mocking voice. "Anyone can see that."

I went even brighter red.

"Course I'm not. I just felt sorry for her, because she's no good at Spit," I said.

The moment the words were out of my mouth, I could have kicked myself. Frankie turned on me. I could see tears in her eyes.

"I don't need your sympathy, Ollie," she said very quietly.

I got up and went out of the room, because it felt like my face had won the reddest tomato of the year competition. Rory, the toerag, followed me all the way upstairs.

"I'm going to the washroom, Rory. Do you want to come too?" I asked sarcastically.

"I just came to tell you that whatever you say,

I *know* you're in love with her, because I've heard you saying her name in your sleep. It's so embarrassing."

"Well, it must have been a nightmare if I did," I snapped back at Rory.

Then just when I was on the point of going into the washroom, I saw that Frankie had appeared at the top of the stairs. She must have heard every word.

7. PIGGY IN THE MIDDLE

It didn't take Einstein to work out that Mom had told Rory to get off my case. Ever since the red tomato competition, whenever Mom was around, he acted like he was going for best behaved boy of the year. But the moment we were on our own, he pretended to be playing romantic violin music, giving it the full smoochy sound effects, or otherwise he made some clever little remark like, "Oh, where's your girlfriend, Ollie? Better find her quick in case she's missing you."

"Don't be stupid, Rory. She's practically my sister," I'd snap back at him.

Because of my pathetic little brother, everything had gone wrong. Before he'd started interfering, Frankie and I had been getting on really well together. Now she was all distant and unfriendly. It was unbearable.

On the afternoon of the tragic tournament, we went for miles in the car. Twice we stopped to explore little coastal villages. The pavements were always too narrow for more than two people to walk side by side. I happened to be next to Charlie for quite a while. She did that thing of not stepping on the cracks between the paving stones, but they were a bit too close together, so she had to take stupid little mincing steps. She pretended to be a posh girl wiggling her hips and I couldn't help laughing. But then I felt suddenly sad. I wished it was Frankie and me laughing.

* * *

The following day I woke up and remembered this was the day we were going to meet Sam. It was going to be so weird having Sam around at the same time as Frankie. I wasn't sure that I was looking forward to it. Normally I'd be really pleased about the thought of having a laugh with my best friend, but everything was different now. I just wanted to be with Frankie and no one else.

We were due to meet Sam and his mom outside the Super Discount in Ashbury Park at twelve-thirty and then eat lunch with them, somewhere like McDonald's hopefully. We were a bit late so I guessed they'd get there first. I guessed right.

We all spotted Mrs. Cotteril from miles away. She was wearing a bright pink jacket on top of a pair of black shiny pants with enormous flares. On her head was a whopping great floppy straw hat, and perched on her nose a pair of very little around sunglasses. When you got nearer you could see that her shirt was white with pink spots on it, and the top bit turned into a sort of floaty scarf. Then when you got even nearer you could see little stiletto heels poking out from the bottom of the pants. What did she think she looked like! I didn't know how Sam could bear to be seen with her. I'd have to stand a few feet away from Mom if she ever dressed like that.

"Hell-ooo!" she called, waving both arms in the air as though she was flagging in a Boeing 747.

I noticed poor old Sam trying to grab one of her arms to stop her, but she just shook him off and kept waving.

"Good old Pammy!" said Mom.

"What *have* I let myself in for?" muttered Peter.

Rory giggled and turned to Charlie and Frankie. "Told you Sam was weird, didn't I?

Well, now you know where he gets it from."

Frankie laughed loudly. She wasn't so quick to defend weird people this time, I noticed.

"Hi, Sam. Hello, Mrs. Cotteril," I said.

"Ollie, you must call me Pammy. Are you having a lovely holiday? We are, although we've left my sister Letitia and my niece at home. Poor Daisy isn't feeling a hundred percent today. Still, never mind. I expect you'll meet her another day."

Sam rolled his eyes at me, as Mom and the others arrived. Sam's mom was staring at Frankie and Charlie with this really silly smile on her face, even though she was talking to Mom.

"Hello, Sue. You're looking tanned. Not good for you, you know. It'll ruin your skin, not to mention the health hazard. But it *does* suit you, my dear, I must confess. And who are these two lovely young ladies?"

"This is Frankie and this is Charlie," said

Mom. But Mrs. Cotteril was nodding and waiting for more.

"Peter's daughters," Mom explained.

Frankie and Charlie smiled dutifully.

"Hello, my dears."

"You've met Peter before, haven't you, Pammy?" said Mom.

"Oh yes, yes yes," said Mrs. C, wafting her hand about as though she was trying to get rid of Mom's silly remark. "We met at the school fair, didn't we, Peter? I was the one serving the squash, remember?"

Peter smiled and mumbled something.

"Come on, then," she said, as she swung around, narrowly missing Rory's head with her handbag. (Too bad.) Then she went striding through the crowded street, like a big pink plow, while we all followed meekly. "I've found us the most super little restaurant within walking distance, and reserved a table . . ." She stopped without warning to look at her watch, and I walked into the back of her. I could hear Sam snickering and the others trying to hide their giggles. Great start! Mrs. Cotteril didn't appear to notice, and I must admit her back felt very spongy. Perhaps she wore body protection. "Twelve thirty-five. Perfect timing." Then off she went again, left right, left right.

The restaurant was really fancy.

"Mom always chooses places like this," said Sam in a whisper to me. It was amazing that he didn't care. If it had been my mom I would have been dead embarrassed if we went anywhere that looked much different from McDonald's.

I saw Mom give Peter a worried look. I knew why. She was feeling anxious that it might be too expensive. She opened her mouth to say something, then shut it again and shrugged as Mrs. Cotteril marched up to a waiter and told him she'd booked a table for twelve forty-five. Our table was right in the middle of the whole restaurant. We were on the point of sitting down, when the foghorn started laying down the law.

"Come on, you two. You're not going to leave these beautiful young ladies with no young men to sit next to, are you? Let Frankie pop in next to you, Sam . . ."

Sam looked as though the thought of sitting next to Frankie was the scariest thing ever. He wasn't used to girls any more than I was, and I knew he'd hate having to sit next to her. I was praying that Mrs. C would suggest that I should sit next to her instead, but I was out of luck.

"I'm fine, honestly," said Frankie.

"Nonsense. Move up one, Sam."

Sam stayed glued to me but shoved me along one, so Frankie could sit in the seat between him and Peter.

Mrs. Cotteril was smiling and patting the chair next to her. "You come and sit next to me, Sue. I want to hear what you've been getting up to."

Mom was staring at the pepper like she was willing it to give her a bit of help. She needn't have bothered. Sam's mom was beaming around at us all.

"Lovely!" she said, taking her jacket off. "Just how it should be – boy, girl, boy, girl . . . apart from those two naughty boys sitting together over there."

"That's because of those two naughty girls sitting together over there," said Charlie, pointing to Mrs. Cotteril and Mom.

Peter closed his eyes as though he couldn't bear to see what was going to happen after his daughter's cheeky remark. Mrs. Cotteril's eyes bulged. I don't suppose anyone had ever dared to speak to her like that before. We all held our breath and after a couple of seconds she suddenly let out a great guffaw of laughter and wagged her finger at Charlie.

"I can see you're going to be a terror!" she exclaimed, which made Rory break into uncontrollable giggles.

But the moment passed quickly. Mrs. C held her pink jacket aloft.

"Waiter!" In about two seconds a waiter appeared and took the jacket. "You can always tell how good a restaurant is by the attitude of the waiters, you know," she whispered to Peter. She'd swapped her sunglasses for a pair of half glasses hanging on a sparkling string. She looked over the top of them at Mom.

"This meal is on me, my dear." Mom started to protest, but Mrs. Cotteril flapped Mom's words away again. "No, no, no. I'm having none of it. I want to treat you all because I have a favor to ask you." I saw Mom gulp. "There's an absolutely super concert on tomorrow afternoon at the Dominion, and my sister's next-door neighbor's brother-in-law is the conductor, which is so exciting. Of course the youngsters would frankly be bored to tears. So . . . we were wondering whether you and Peter might be so kind as to have Sam and Daisy for us."

"Yes, of course we will," Mom said immediately. She looked quite relieved. She must have been imagining a much bigger favor.

"Wonderful. That's settled, then. Daisy will be fine tomorrow. She's had a touch of sickness and diarrhea but nothing to worry about."

"What's Daisy like?" Frankie asked Sam.

"She's all right," Sam muttered, then he buried his head in the menu.

"Yes, but what's she *like*?" Frankie persisted.

"She's got short hair," said Sam. This time he practically turned his back on Frankie, he was so embarrassed about talking to a girl. It was quite funny really.

"How old is she and what kind of things does she like doing?" Frankie leaned forwards and a big strand of her hair fell over Sam's shoulder. I saw him look at it out of the corner of his eye, and then try to pull his shoulder away subtly.

"Thirteen. Hockey," was all he managed.

On the other side of me Charlie and Rory were giggling together about something – probably Sam.

"And what about you?" Frankie said to Sam, touching his arm for a second, to try and get him to face her a bit more, but it just made him jump.

Just then Peter chipped in.

"What are we going to do tomorrow then, you guys? Got any ideas, Sam?"

Sam looked at Peter as though he'd just saved him from a man-eating alligator. "Ten-pin bowling?" he piped up.

Yeah! That would be great.

"Ten-pin bowling?" said Peter. "You any good at it, Sam?"

"He's a super little bowler!" said Mrs. Cotteril, which made Charlie's menu shake up and down in front of her face, but Mrs. C didn't even notice.

"Right, bowling it is," said Peter. "We'll have boys against girls."

"And we'll slaughter them, won't we, girls?" said Mom.

"Yeah!" said Charlie, showing a pink face and watering eyes. I was right. She'd been having hysterics behind her menu.

"Whereabouts in Ashbury Park are you staying, Sam?" Frankie went on, tossing her head so her hair went back over her shoulder.

And I suddenly got that same feeling that I'd had when those two boys had looked at her on the beach. I knew it was stupid, because it was only Sam, but I couldn't help feeling jealous.

Frankie was being so friendly with him, and I knew he'd start to get used to it after a bit. Then it was anyone's guess what might happen. If Frankie carried on draping her hair all over him, he might get the idea she was interested in him. The very thought of that made my blood boil.

I wished we could get this stupid meal over with, and go home. Then I remembered about having to see him the next day. The whole thing was turning into a nightmare. If only Frankie would stop giving Sam so much attention! It was like she was doing it on purpose.

"That's a very fierce scowl, Oliver," Mrs. Cotteril suddenly broke off what she was saying to Mom to tell me.

I was already pretty mad, but that did it. It was bad enough having all these mixed-up feelings about Frankie, but I didn't want the whole world watching every single expression I ever wore.

Good old Peter said something about Rory

and Charlie's sandcastles then, and it got Mrs. Cotteril off my case.

But I could see Sam getting more and more mesmerized by Frankie's hair. Too bad she hadn't got it up in one of those big scrunchie things. He finally stopped gaping and answered her question.

"At my Aunt Letitia's. She's divorced, you see." He made it sound a really terrible thing to be. Frankie was nodding sympathetically, as though he'd just said she was terminally ill or something. Sam *did* have a dad, but he wasn't around much because he worked out of state.

"Loads of people are divorced these days," I informed Sam.

"So whereabouts does Aunt Letitia live?" Frankie carried on, ignoring me.

She and Sam were acting like I wasn't there. Maybe I'd died without realizing it, and turned into a ghost.

"She's got an apartment on Webb Street. Number 4. She lives on the second floor. You have to take the elevator."

He'd be giving her his phone number next, the idiot!

After that, things went downhill all the way. All that I'd imagined, started coming true. Frankie talked more and more to Sam until he wasn't nervous of her at all. He was looking right into her eyes and cracking all sorts of clever jokes, while she giggled and looked at him from under her straight eyelashes. I nearly threw up.

To make matters worse, while those two were talking like mad on one side of me, Charlie and Rory were giggling like mad on the other side. I felt like poor sad piggy in the middle. Mrs. Cotteril kept on trying to draw me into the adults' conversation, which stopped me from being able to hear what Frankie and Sam were saying to each other, and that made me more jealous than ever. I don't know why I ever thought Sam was my best friend. He certainly wasn't any more.

8. SCHEMING

It came as a big relief when Mrs. Cotteril looked at her watch and said, "Oh my goodness, three-thirty! How time flies when you're enjoying yourself."

She paid the bill and we all thanked her very much.

"Oh no, no, no! It's *I* who must thank *you* for looking after the young folk tomorrow. Waiter?" We followed her out of the restaurant and stood in a line waiting to be kissed on both cheeks. There was no way out of it. She'd done it to

Mom, Peter and Frankie so far. Talk about embarrassing! When it got to my turn I braced myself and turned my head really far to the side so her lips wouldn't reach properly. My technique worked: I was the only one who didn't have to rub the greasy pink mark off my face when she'd gone.

"Bye, Frankie," said Sam in a gooey voice.

"See you tomorrow, Sam," Frankie replied, tipping her head on one side and flashing him one of her really nice smiles.

Sam looked as though the Angel Gabriel had appeared and pronounced him the chosen one. It was amazing that one girl could have this effect. Not only had she got Sam *and* me thinking she was the greatest thing on God's earth, she'd got me hating my friend's guts too. Maybe that's what girl power means.

"Bye Sam," I said loudly to bring him back to earth, but his eyes were still glued to Frankie.

"Yeah, seeya, Ollie."

Not if I can help it!

From that moment on I was determined that somehow or other I was going to make sure that tomorrow afternoon never happened. I just couldn't stomach spending another second with Sam and Frankie hitting it off so well while I felt like a spare part. I spent the rest of the afternoon scheming. By the time we got back home I figured I'd come up with something that, with a bit of luck, would work like a charm. I was going to pretend to be ill.

Next I had to decide on the illness. I didn't want to get everyone so worried that they started calling doctors or ambulances or anything like that, because I guessed medical people would know there was nothing wrong with me pretty quickly. On the other hand I needed to be ill enough for Mom and Peter to be pretty anxious and feel very sorry for me. The good thing about this idea was that Frankie would be sorry for me too — so sorry that she'd forget all about my ex-friend Sam Cotteril.

Right, what was the illness to be? Food poisoning was probably the best idea because I could blame it on the meal we'd had in that fancy restaurant. Except I wasn't sure when the poisoning would have started. Maybe I should wait till just after the pizza and fries that Mom was about to pull out of the freezer. No, that wouldn't work. With two large pizzas between six of us, the others would be poisoned as well.

I racked my brains to think of a solution, and it was Charlie who gave me my next bit of inspiration.

"I'm really full, Sue. I don't think I can manage pizza and fries after that big lunch and the ice cream in the park."

"Yeah, I'm full too, Mom," I said. "Why don't

we just have sandwiches in front of the TV? I don't mind making them."

Mom beamed at me. *Ten out of ten, Ollie.*

"Good idea, Ollie. Go for it!" She frowned. "Wait a minute, what have we got to put in sandwiches?"

"We've got eggs and cheese and jam, haven't we?" I pointed out helpfully. "I'll just make a selection," I offered. "How long are you supposed to boil the eggs for?"

"Turn the heat down when the water's boiled and leave them in for about ten minutes to be sure. Then put them in cold water to cool down before you shell them."

As I went through to the kitchen I felt like singing because Frankie had almost smiled at me. At this rate I wouldn't need to be ill. I'd just keep impressing her with my helpful-boy-of-the-century act. My plan was to hardboil two eggs so there wouldn't be many egg sandwiches.

I'd do a lot more cheese and jam ones, but only eat the egg ones myself. That way, it would be perfectly possible that one of the eggs was rotten and that by coincidence I'd just happened to be the only one to eat sandwiches made from that egg. Brilliant! And utterly foolproof. I *did* start singing then, I felt so good.

"There you go," I said a bit later, as I put the big platter down on the coffee table.

They were all engrossed in the television, but Mom gave me a nice smile and mouthed *Well done*.

I was hoping that Frankie might give me a nice smile too, but she just looked irritated because I was blocking the screen from her view. Talk about gratitude. Huh!

I quickly took three egg sandwiches and put them on my plate, then I thought I ought to draw attention to what I was eating, so that when I started writhing around with stomach cramps in about twenty minutes, everyone would instantly make the connection.

"Don't take all the egg ones," said Rory, who'd been the only one paying more attention to the sandwiches than to the TV.

The perfect opening. Cheers, Rory.

"Anyone want some tea?" I asked when all the sandwiches had gone.

"Yes please," said Mom, with another big beam.

Peter winked at me and Charlie pretended to faint.

"No thanks," said Frankie. "But I'll help you make it if you want."

It was like a nature reserve inside my stomach, there were so many butterflies zooming about.

"Thanks."

She followed me into the kitchen and we started getting all the tea things out, neither of us speaking. I wished I could get inside her head and find out whether she was thinking about Sam or me or what. This was the perfect situation to start acting ill, but I felt nervous all of a sudden. I didn't like the idea of deceiving Frankie. Still, it was all in a good cause.

"Aargh!"

"What . . . ?"

I gripped the sink with both hands and lowered my head.

"Are you all right?"

"Yeah . . . yeah . . . I'll be OK. It felt like a stomach cramp . . . Aargh!"

I made that second cry a bit more dramatic, but I didn't clutch my stomach or anything. I wanted to bring it on gradually.

"Are you all right in there?" called Mom from the other room.

"Ollie's got a stomach ache," Frankie called back.

No one came rushing to my aid, I noticed.

It's great having such a loyal fan club!

I poured the boiling water on to the tea and deliberately made my hand shake as I was doing it. Out of the corner of my eye I could see the worried look on Frankie's face.

"You'd better sit down, Ollie. I'll finish off the tea."

I went through to the other room then staggered past Mom, murmuring that I was going to the washroom.

She didn't say anything, but looked pretty concerned. So far, so good.

While I was in the bathroom I ran the hot water and hung my face over the rising steam with a towel over my head, for ages. When I looked in the mirror it looked just right. I'd got a sort of sweaty red glow. I belted downstairs really quickly before it went, then slowed right down for my entrance into the living-room. It still wasn't quite time to clutch my stomach, but

I thought a bit of reeling around on my way to the couch would be good.

"I was nearly sick," I told Mom weakly as I flopped back on to the couch.

That got her attention. She sat up quickly and examined my face carefully.

"My God, you're sweating, Ollie!"

"You look terrible!" Charlie added, screwing up her face into a disgusted expression.

"Have you still got stomach cramps?" asked Frankie.

I nodded and closed my eyes as though the pain was too much to bear.

Rory wasn't saying anything, I noticed, which either meant that he was so worried about his dearly beloved brother that he'd been rendered speechless, or he wasn't convinced by my act and he was watching me like a hawk, ready to bust my cover at the first opportunity.

Still, so far so good.

9. SICK!

I hadn't felt such power since I'd broken my arm in the school playground and all the teachers had gathered around me and spoken in gentle, caring tones. I had to be careful though. If I got busted, I'd have to suffer watching Sam and Frankie hitting it off like Prince Charming and Cinderella, *and* get a load of grief from Mom.

Mom kept on reaching out to feel how hot I was.

"That's better," she said after a while. "You don't

seem to have such a temperature now. I was quite worried there for a while."

And that got me worried. I didn't want to overdo it and pretend to be sick too often, or I'd get figured out, but on the other hand, I had to appear to be ill enough to screw up the arrangements for the next day, I decided another trip to the bathroom was about due.

"I feel sick again!" I said, making a dive for the door and rushing upstairs.

I ran another sink full of really hot water and went through the towel routine again to get that sweaty look back, then I was ready.

"Have you been sick?" asked Mom sympathetically when I reappeared.

I wasn't sure if Mom would take one sniff and know straight away that I was lying, so I knew I had to be careful.

"A bit," I answered in a whisper as I sunk dramatically into the couch.

"You'd better try and drink a bit of water," said Mom. "You must be quite dehydrated."

I sipped at the water but kept my eyes shut as though I was exhausted. Actually, I *was* exhausted. It wasn't easy keeping the act up with so many people watching me. Rory looked as though he wasn't quite convinced, for a start. But I knew how my little brother's mind worked. He'd be thinking that he'd better not accuse me of faking it, just in case he was wrong, because then everyone would hate him for being so hard on me.

I was also worn out from trying to keep an eye on Frankie without anyone noticing. The last thing I wanted was to make her dislike me even more, but it's not easy to look burning hot *and* super-cool at the same time. I kept my eyes closed because I had the horrible feeling Rory was trying to find me out. I wished he'd just go to bed or something.

"What are we going to do if Ollie's still not well tomorrow?" Charlie asked the six million dollar question.

"We'll cross that bridge when we come to it," Mom replied. "I think you should go to bed now, dear," she said to me, stroking my hair off my face.

I felt pretty smug as I lay in bed, staring into the darkness. I just had to show no signs of improvement in the morning, and hopefully the whole trip would be called off. I could hear them all killing themselves laughing at something on the TV, and I wished I was down there too, but I thought it was worth giving up one evening to make sure I didn't have to suffer the company of Romeo and Juliet the next day.

I was suddenly aware of whispering and tiptoeing around me. I listened for a while with my eyes closed, while the memory of the previous evening slowly came back to me. We'd finally arrived at that awful day. I gave a little moan and turned over.

"How do you feel?" asked Mom, sitting on my bed and stroking my forehead. "I don't think you've got a temperature, so that's a good start."

"My head aches," I whispered, "and so does my stomach."

I half opened my eyes and saw that Rory and Charlie were hovering in the doorway, waiting for the verdict.

"Do you want to get up and see how you feel, dear?"

"I'll try," I said, wishing that Rory and Charlie would go away. It was so much easier fooling Mom on her own.

"I'll be downstairs. Just call out if you want me."

She shooed Rory and Charlie away as she went out, but I made sure I got out of bed very slowly and with a pained expression on my face just in case Antenna-Head was peeping through the crack in the door. When I went to the bathroom I could hear that they were all talking in hushed voices downstairs but I couldn't make out what they were saying. I looked in the mirror and thought I looked far too healthy and normal. I went back to bed and got down under the covers so that only the top half of my face was showing, then I called out to Mom in a really pathetic voice.

She came running up straight away and sat down on the bed.

"I tried getting up, Mom, but I haven't got any energy. I think it's because I was sick once more during the night. I'll be OK by tomorrow, but I'd better stay in bed today."

"OK, dear. You know how you feel. I'll stay with you."

"What do you mean?"

"Don't worry about me, Ollie. I wasn't all that excited about going bowling anyway. The others can go on their own and I'll have some quiet time to myself for reading. I'm looking forward to it. Honestly."

She was nodding and smiling brightly to reassure me that she really didn't mind having to drop out of the great outing to the Ashbury Bowlplex. And I was lying there, my brain in overdrive trying to think how I could rewind the morning and wake up again, miraculously cured. I wanted to kick myself for being such an idiot. I should have realized they'd all just go bowling anyway, shouldn't I?

I couldn't bear the thought of Sam and Frankie there without me. Her eyelashes'd be batting so much, she'd probably get eye ache — and as for Sam, well, he'd just act like a complete idiot. I had to do something. And quick.

"Well, I might feel better by this afternoon.

We're not meeting them till then, are we?"

"No, but Peter thought it would be nice to have a look around the town beforehand and maybe go to McDonald's at lunchtime."

What was she trying to do, torture me?

"I'm just going to the bathroom, Mom."

I got out of bed slowly and went off to the bathroom. Then I cleaned my teeth and washed my face. By the time I got back to my room Mom was downstairs. I got dressed and went down too.

"I feel a lot better now I've had a wash," I said, smiling around at everyone.

"That's good," said Peter. "By tomorrow you'll be completely cured I should think. Just take it easy today. Your body must be quite weakened with all that vomiting."

"Well, it was only twice and the second time there was hardly anything."

"Wonderful, Ollie!" said Rory, who was in the

living-room eating a piece of toast and kicking a ball of screwed-up newspaper around the room. "Why don't you give me all the gory details, so I can *really* enjoy this toast."

I ignored him.

"It's amazing. The weakness seems to have gone now,' I said, as I went into to the kitchen. "Is there any toast left, Mom?"

"Are you sure you feel like eating, Ollie?"

"Yeah! I'm starving," I grinned.

"You *are* feeling better!" She turned to Peter. "I think as long as he takes it easy, he'll be all right to come along, don't you?"

"If Ollie thinks he can cope, I'm sure he can."

Phew!

10. BOWLED OVER!

We weren't due to meet Sam and Daisy until two-thirty so we went out for the morning to a town about five miles away, where they had crazy golf, pedal boats and various rides. We had a great time – correction, everyone else had a great time. I'd only been allowed to come on condition that I didn't do any of the white-knuckle rides. I begged and begged to be allowed to go in a bumper car and said I was feeling much better, but Mom still wouldn't let me. The biggest torture was watching Frankie and Charlie going down this massive slide together in a sack, laughing their heads off. A few days ago that would have been Frankie and me.

Someone next to me said, "Look at those pretty blonde girls. Do you think they're twins?" I felt proud for a moment that they were my step-sisters, and then I felt all confused again because I wished that Frankie could be my girlfriend.

The miracle happened when she said she'd ride in the ghost train with me. It was wicked because twice she grabbed hold of me when something scary suddenly jumped out at us. I nearly put my arm around her but I thought that might be overdoing it a bit. I wasn't sure if it was OK for a stepbrother to do things like that. I wanted to suggest that we had another go in the ghost train, but I could just hear Rory's scornful voice . . . *Ollie got better quickly, didn't he?*

When we got to the Bowlplex there was no sign of Sam and Daisy. Maybe they wouldn't show up at all. (Yeah, right. And maybe Ashbury Bowlplex would freeze over.) Peter bought the tickets and we changed into bowling shoes and went to our lane. The man at the desk had asked us if we wanted bumpers up the sides of the lane. Mom said she thought it might be an idea as Charlie, Frankie and Rory had never played before, and I'd only played once, but we'd all insisted that we weren't babies and that we *did* know how to roll the balls accurately down the middle.

Frankie and Charlie were engrossed in setting up all the names on the computer screen that kept the score.

"How shall we organize the teams, Sue?" asked Frankie.

And that was when we heard, "Hell-ooo!"

We turned to see Mrs. Cotteril in a bright

green pantsuit that was even bigger and floatier than yesterday's clothes. Standing next to her was a lady with white-blonde hair that looked as though it had been pasted on to the top of her head in thick chunks. She was just as huge as Sam's mom and was wearing a big gold jacket and tons of gold jewelry.

She must be Mrs. Cotteril's sister, I thought. *Poor old Sam, having to walk around with two of them like that!*

"They look like a pair of Spanish galleons in full sail," Peter whispered in a voice just loud enough for all of us to hear.

Mom cracked up and then had to make out that it was a fit of coughing. The rest of us snickered and pretended to be concentrating on the score screen. When we turned back around Sam and this dorky looking girl were approaching us, while Sam's mom jabbed her watch then held up five fingers and a thumb.

She was obviously coming back at six o'clock.

Mom gave her the thumbs-up sign, then the Spanish galleons waved and departed.

"Hello, you must be Daisy," said Mom, because Sam wasn't bothering to introduce her. He was asking about the teams, like it was the draw for a cup final.

"You need to change your shoes, Sam," Frankie told him. "I'll take you."

"I — oh, thanks!"

He was about to say *I know* but he changed his mind so that he could go with Frankie.

Here we go!

I watched them walk over to the desk. Frankie's hair was half up and half down, the way I liked it best. There was something different about Sam and I wasn't sure what it was at first.

"This is Daisy," Mom said, smiling at Charlie and me.

"Hello," we all said.

I couldn't believe that Daisy was thirteen. She looked like an oversized nine-year-old. She kind of bunched up her shoulders and tucked her head in, like a tortoise. She had very pink shiny cheeks and short hair.

"I'll take you to change your shoes," said Charlie.

What a relief. I wouldn't have had a clue what to say to Daisy if it had been me. We'd have walked in silence all the way to the desk and all the way back. I noticed that she'd put lipstick on and she'd got glitter all around her eyes. I suppose I could have said something like, "Oh, I see you've got glitter on," but then she'd have said, "Yes", and that would have been the end of that.

The sight of Sam and Frankie coming back really *did* make me feel like throwing up. Sam was kind of bobbing up and down in his brand new jeans, and both of them were chatting like they had to say as much as possible in sixty seconds. Maybe they'd discussed me and were laughing together about what a dweeb I was, falling for my own stepsister.

"How you doing, Ollie?"

I didn't bother to reply because it was obvious he wasn't interested in how I was doing. It didn't even sound like Sam talking. He was trying to be so cool.

"Right, let's get these teams organized," said Peter, as Daisy and Charlie came back. "Shall we toss a coin?"

I held my breath and prayed. And that was a waste of time because it came out that I was with Charlie, Mom and Daisy. Great! So the other team was Peter, Rory, Frankie and Sam. I was definitely going to suggest swapping the teams around for the next game.

Rory went first and his ball missed the pins

altogether and rolled down the gutter at the side of the lane.

"I knew we should have had bumpers," said Mom.

"That was only my first turn. I'll be fine," said Rory.

Everyone had two turns. Rory's second one wasn't much better – three pins.

Next it was Charlie because we were going from youngest to oldest. Like Rory, she missed all the pins the first time. On her second try, she knocked down two.

"High scoring game!" joked Peter. "Who's next?"

"When's your birthday, Sam?" Frankie asked him.

"November the twenty-sixth," said Sam.

"What an incredible coincidence!" said Frankie. "Mine's the twenty-seventh! I'm one day younger than you, so I go first."

Oh, terrific!

"Actually, it's a proven statistic that in any group of eight people, there'll usually be two people with exactly the same birthday, so it's not that much of a coincidence," I told them sourly. They just ignored me.

Frankie took her run up with the ball. She sent it really hard and it knocked down eight of the pins. When she turned around she looked a bit embarrassed because she'd done so well.

"Yesss!" said Sam, punching the air. "Wow! I thought *I* was good at it . . ."

Why didn't he just put a sock in it?

"Who's older out of you two?" asked Charlie, looking at me and Daisy. Daisy lifted her shoulders and buried her head again as though she was too shy to say her age. I felt as though I was years older than her. It was quite insulting to think she was thirteen.

"My birthday's in February," I said a bit

snappily. I didn't want to say the exact date because people always made jokes about it.

"So is mine!" said Daisy, her head poking right out of its shell and a big grin appearing on her shiny face. "What date's yours?"

"Fourteenth," I mumbled.

"Oh, mine's the twenty-third."

"You go next then."

"The postman thinks Ollie's really popular when he delivers all these cards on Valentine's Day," Sam told Frankie with a grin.

Frankie giggled. I ignored her and watched Daisy. She had the wrong foot in front, she didn't bend down properly, she didn't follow through and the ball trickled along as though it was entering the slowest ball of the year competition. By a miracle it clipped one of the pins.

"One better than me," said Charlie, smiling at Daisy. "I think it's going to be up to Ollie and

Sue to get the points for our team."

Daisy's second try was exactly the same as her first.

"At least you're consistent," said Peter.

"Right, my turn," said Sam, picking up one of the really heavy balls.

"Whoa! A professional!" Peter said, eyeing the ball.

Sam grinned and took his throw. It went straight down the middle and knocked over every single pin.

"Strike!" said Frankie, jumping up and down. "You're really great at it, Sam!"

Sam was wearing this over-the-top cool expression that he'd probably been practicing in front of the mirror. I felt the approach of another severe attack of nausea.

"Your turn, Ollie," said Charlie.

My heart was beating fast. I'd feel so stupid if I didn't knock at least six down. I decided to take a heavy ball like Sam's, because it looked like they were the best. I threw the ball as hard as I could, which hurt my hand, but at least it rolled fast. It was pretty straight too. Seven pins went down. Mom clapped and Daisy said, "Good one, Ollie!"

I didn't look at anyone, just took my other shot and prayed. The remaining three pins were all knocked down.

"A spare! That's great, Ollie," said Charlie. "Our team stands a chance, after all."

Mom and Peter both scored eleven, so the game was looking pretty even. And that's the way it carried on. Except that Sam went from strength to strength. How could he be so good at bowling when he was useless at every other sport? The trouble was, he *knew* he was impressing everyone and it made him even more cocky. He was hardly recognizable as Sam Cotteril. He was acting more like Justin

Timberlake. And it was pretty obvious it was all for Frankie's benefit.

There was only one thing for it. I'd have to have a word with the Almighty. I'd never believed in proper praying before, but I was feeling desperate, and if I had to watch Frankie smiling and jumping up and down one more time because Sam had played yet another good shot, I'd go around the bend.

I made it look like I was studying the scores on the computer screen, but really I was saying this prayer:

Dear God, I know you're probably busy, but if you could possibly take a glance at Ashbury Bowlplex I'd be really grateful. You'll notice that there's a boy in lane 4 who needs some help to stop him being so vain. Could you please arrange it for him to throw the next few balls so badly that he doesn't knock a single pin down?

This will make him much more . . . kind of humble, you know. Sorry I haven't been all that good at praying until now, but I promise I'll pray twice a day forever if you could do this for me. Thank you very much. Amen.

Then I waited. Apart from Rory, Daisy was the only one whose game improved. She'd started off looking and playing like a giant tortoise, but after five or six turns she was almost as good as Sam. Peter had spent ages trying to help her to stand properly and showing her how to follow through, and it had paid off.

I was stunned when she got her first strike.

"Wicked, Daisy!"

"Hey thanks, Ollie!" she said — practically the first words she'd spoken to me.

And as I looked at her gooey face two things happened. One: I had a brilliant brainwave, and two: I realized that it's true what people say.

God *does* move in mysterious ways. He must have decided that it would be a bit heavy to blatantly mess up Sam's game, so he'd come up with the cunning idea of me giving Daisy tons of compliments and attention, to make Frankie jealous. Then *she'd* stop drooling all over Sam, and *that* would wipe the stupid grin off Sam's face. Done! I only just stopped myself from laughing out loud.

I waited till Daisy had had her next go and scored a half strike, then said "Yessss!" as I punched the air, just like Sam had done. "Well done, Daisy. I can't believe you never played before today!"

She went bright pink.

"Really? You're not just saying it, are you?"

Out of the corner of my eye I could see Frankie watching me, so I decided I'd pull out all the stops.

"Course not. You're really great."

When I looked back on the whole afternoon I realized that what I'd said was bad enough, but what I did next was a hundred times worse. But once I'd done it, I could hardly take it back. I just had to put up with the sound of my immature little brother's voice whispering to Charlie, "Did you see that? Ollie winked at Daisy!"

Why didn't he go and play on the highway?

11. TORTURE (*CONTINUED*)

After the so-embarrassing wink (oh, why did I go that far?) Daisy wouldn't leave me alone. I know I wanted her to think I liked her, but this was ridiculous! I should have stuck to giving her compliments. As if that wasn't bad enough, every so often Rory'd thrust his stupid grinning face right in front of mine and give me a big wink. I wanted to yell at him but I knew that would only make him do it more, so I had to ignore him, which took a whole lot of self-control, I can tell you.

The first game went on for ages and ages, and in the end Sam's team won. Daisy came and tucked her arm through mine and whispered, "We'll win the next game — just you see!"

I prayed that someone might suggest we change teams, but no such luck. Daisy carried on playing really well. My play was no better and no worse, but Charlie and Mom got loads of strikes, and in the end our team won.

"You don't deserve to be on the losing side, Sam," said Frankie. "You're easily the best player here."

"And Daisy's the most improved player," I added, which made Daisy go all pink and silly.

We'd only booked two games so we went to the arcade afterwards.

"Wanna play a game of air hockey, Ollie?" asked Sam.

Surprise, surprise. He's actually asking me, not Frankie. Wonders will never cease.

We went over to the air hockey table and I was about to put fifty cents in the slot when Sam grabbed my sleeve and came grinning up really close to me.

"She's great, isn't she?" he said, jerking his head very unsubtly in Frankie's direction. "It's incredible. I've never been interested in anyone before, and I think she actually likes me too. She keeps smiling at me."

"No, she acts like that with everyone. She would have told me if she liked you. She tells me everything, you see."

I thought that might take the wind out of his sails, but it was like I hadn't even spoken.

"You're lucky having her as a sister, but on the other hand, I'm glad she's not *my* sister, because then I wouldn't be able to like her like that, would I? I can't wait till I can officially say she's my girlfriend, but first something's got to happen. And it's going to happen tomorrow."

The more he talked, the more I wanted to hit him. The knot was tightening inside my stomach.

"She's not my sister, actually."

"Yeah, but she is in a way, isn't she?"

"No, she's not in any way at all. We haven't got the same mother or the same father."

"Yeah, but your mom's living with her dad, so she's your stepsister, right?"

"That's just a name."

Sam must have got fed up with my arguments, because he quickly changed the subject. "Do you like Daisy?"

"She's OK."

"You're acting like she's fantastic!"

"I was just trying to be nice. She seemed a bit shy."

"Well, she's not shy any more. Look. She's watching you right now."

"Let's just play a game, alright?"

"Don't you want to know what's going to happen tomorrow?"

"Not particularly."

Not for a million bucks.

"I'm going to get Frankie to kiss me."

That did it. I rammed the quarters into the slot and hit the disc so hard that it banged into the sides four times and finished up nearer me than Sam. Sam was getting far too full of himself for my liking. How did he know we were even going to meet up again tomorrow? His eyes goggled behind his glasses as I whacked disc after disc into the sides at about eighty miles per hour and won the game fourteen-zilch in two minutes flat.

I wondered if he was planning on taking those glasses off when he kissed Frankie. What a thought! I had to shake it out of my head before it took root. Unfortunately I was too late, because it came back to me about three times a minute, gutting me every time.

Frankie and Daisy came over when we finished our game.

"It'd be great if we could get together again tomorrow," said Daisy. "It's so boring with Mom and Pammy, isn't it, Sam?"

"My mom's made other arrangements for tomorrow," I said.

"Like what?" asked Frankie.

"If it's nice, we're going to the beach," I told her.

"What if it's not nice?" asked Daisy.

"We're going out for the day," I answered.

Mom hadn't said a word about what we were going to do the next day, but nobody needed to know that.

"Do you think they'd mind if we came along too?" asked Daisy.

If my body had been a balloon, that remark would have made all the air go out of me. I couldn't be bothered to reply. I just wandered back to the others so I didn't hear how Frankie answered. One thing was certain though. No way was I going to spend another day with Sam and Daisy. It was too much effort pretending that I thought Daisy was a Britney Spears lookalike. There was no point anyway – Frankie obviously liked Sam better than me. All I could do was try and make sure we didn't see him and Daisy any more this holiday. At least then I'd get Frankie back to myself, even if she didn't actually like me as much as him.

"Can Daisy and Sam come with us to the beach tomorrow?" Charlie asked Mom a bit later.

"Well, that's up to Pammy, and Daisy's mom. It's fine as far as I'm concerned. Is that where you want to go then, the beach?"

"I thought that was what you'd arranged."

Uh-oh! Diversion tactics needed.

"Oh look! There's your mom now, Sam!"

Everyone turned towards the door with welcoming smiles on their faces, and then all the smiles turned to looks of puzzlement as one by one they all turned back to me.

"Where?"

"Oh, sorry, I thought it was that woman there . . ."

"So you think my mom looks like her?" said Sam, grinning. "I must tell Mom when she arrives. She'll be really flattered to know that Ollie got her mixed up with a tall, slim black woman carrying a baby."

Daisy's face was one big frown. I knew what she was doing. She was wildly searching her mind for something to say to make me look less of a dipstick. I wished she wouldn't bother.

"I can see what Ollie means. It's that orange turban thing on her head, because your mom does wear a lot of orange, doesn't she, Sam?"

Of course everyone cracked up when she said that. Rory gave me another of his unsubtle winks then spoke to me behind his hand – the sickening little maggot.

"See your *girlfriend's* sticking up for you, Ollie. Pity Sam's after your other girlfriend, isn't it?"

"I couldn't care less," I said.

"You *could* care less," went on the ruthless turd. "It's obvious you're jealous. That's the only reason you're being nice to Daisy."

He'd only got it sickeningly right again, hadn't he? Was the kid psychic or something?

"Don't talk garbage!"

Suddenly everyone was standing up. While Rory had been giving me severe earache, neither of us had noticed that Mrs. C and Daisy's mom really had arrived. I expect everyone else in the place had noticed though, because they were sailing towards us, arms flying everywhere, big voices booming about the 'magnificent' concert.

"My dears, it was super! Absolutely *sooooooper!* You really should have been there," began Daisy's mom.

We went through the exit turnstiles to join them in the lobby.

"Oh, to sit in that audience, knowing that we had connections with the conductor, was just heavenly!" added Sam's mom, which was a weird thing to say, because she was about as connected to that conductor as I was to the Pope.

"Can Sam and I spend tomorrow with Ollie and everyone, Mommy?" asked Daisy.

My whole body groaned. If only I could rewind and start again from before that stupid wink!

"We'd love to have them," smiled Mom.

"Well, if you're sure it's not too much trouble . . ." said Mrs. Cotteril, giving her sister a sidelong look, which meant *Great! Looks like we can have some more sooooper fun without the children, darling!*

"Well, that's settled," said Mom. "We're going to the beach as long as it's not pouring rain or blowing a gale. So they'll need swimming things."

"Would it be easiest if we drop Sam and Daisy at your holiday home?"

"Why not just meet us on the beach?" said Peter. "I've heard two or three people saying it's going to be lovely and hot again tomorrow."

"Good idea," said Mom. Then she went to great lengths to explain exactly which bit of which beach. "It might be an idea to exchange phone numbers. We'll take our cell-phone with us."

"*Soooper!*" said Pammy as she scribbled on a bit of paper and handed it to Mom. "What time will you be there?"

"By ten, so let's say any time after that."

Then next thing I knew, Daisy's hot breath was right inside my earhole.

"One minute past, then!"

I forced myself to grin at her incredible wit, then wiped my ear as soon as they were all safely out of view.

Little did she know that plan B was about to be put into action.

12. THE NIGHTMARE BEGINS

At seven o'clock the following morning I was crouching behind the hedge on the other side of the road from our house, Mom's cell-phone in my hand and the bit of paper with Sam's aunt's number on it in my pocket. I'd been dreading not waking up early enough, but I needn't have worried. I'd woken up at six-thirty. Mom and Peter normally got up much later than that, so at least I wouldn't get caught in the act. I was as nervous as hell, but it had to be done.

I knew it was rather early to be phoning, but

it was vital that the whole thing sounded as realistic as possible and I reckoned Mom would have given Mrs. C and her sister plenty of notice about our arrangements being altered. I got out the piece of paper that I'd snuck from Mom's bag last night, and punched in the number with shaky fingers. After a few seconds it started ringing, then my legs started shaking too, probably because I was crouching, but I couldn't stand up in case my head showed over the hedge. I covered the mouthpiece and practiced Mom's voice for the fiftieth time.

After eight rings the answering machine message came on. At least I thought it was the answering machine. It was hard to tell because the voice kept on cutting out. I'd never thought of this happening and I began to panic a bit. I was about to disconnect, when Daisy's mom came on the line.

"Hello." She sounded as though she'd been

asleep.

This was it!

"Hello, Letitia. It's Sue Cranshaw here." I'd heard Mom say "Bye, Letitia" yesterday so I knew they were on first name terms.

"Sorry . . . the line's breaking up. *Who* is it?" Great! She couldn't hear my voice properly. Less chance of getting caught.

"I'm so sorry to disturb you at this ungodly hour —" (I liked that bit) — "but I'm afraid Rory and Frankie are unwell, so we'll have to cancel today's arrangements."

The effort of trying to make my voice sound like Mom's was making me sweat. Also, the tremble in my legs seemed to have spread to my voice.

"Oh Sue . . . Sorry, the line's very bad . . . Rory and Frankie what?"

"They're not well."

"Oh, what a bore!"

"I'm going to have to cancel today."

"Sorry, I missed that completely. Say again . . ."

"I'm going to have to cancel today," I tried not to shout.

"Cancel? Oh, what an awful bore for you. Is it runny tummy? That's what Daisy had, you know."

Daisy! Of course! I never thought of that. "I think they probably caught it off Daisy."

"I can hardly hear you, Sue, so I'll say bye bye now. Do give everyone our love. Hope they're better soon."

"Yes. Bye."

I didn't even wait for her answer, just disconnected and felt like dancing around the field, I was so happy. We wouldn't be bothered by Kissing Sam and his hot-breathed cousin any more! All I had to do was smuggle the phone back in before Mom noticed it was missing – which ought to be a piece of cake – and then act as surprised as everyone else when Sam and Daisy didn't show up.

"Coming, Frankie?" I asked.

It was just like it used to be. Charlie and Rory were already digging away, talking about making the biggest moat ever, because there were so few people on the beach, as we'd got there quite early. Mom was lying on her stomach and Peter was rubbing cream into her back. Frankie was scrunching her hair up and I was clutching both the body boards.

"Here, let me take one of them."
As we were running down to the ocean, which was quite far out again, I felt full of hope that today would be the day that would make everything go back to normal. We were just getting into the ocean, when Frankie spoilt my lovely feeling by mentioning Sam.

"Is Sam as good at swimming as he is at bowling?"

I tried not to let it show, but she'd really rattled my cage. You see, if she was *talking* about Sam, then she must have been *thinking* about him.

"Nah. Useless. He hates getting wet. He can't even swim."

That wasn't strictly true. Sam *had* learnt to swim but only just. I didn't think he'd want to do more than paddle in the ocean. Whenever we had swimming at school last year he always stayed at the shallow end. He could swim widths, but he'd never dare attempt a length because that would mean going up to the deep end.

Frankie looked sympathetic.

"Poor old Sam. What about Daisy?"

"I've no idea — oh, wait a minute, she did say something about winning a diving competition."

Frankie didn't make any comment. It was

obvious she didn't believe me. I don't know why I said it really. We were well into the ocean by then and a big wave was coming up behind us.

"Race you!" I said.

It was a close one. She won by about half a yard.

"I haven't lost my touch!" she grinned, and that other horrible conversation seemed to vanish.

For about forty minutes we had a lot of fun. And then:

"It's weird that they haven't shown up yet, isn't it?" said Frankie.

"I bet their mothers take ages and ages getting ready to go out."

"Oh no! My scrunchie's come off. My hair's getting sopping wet."

"It can't have gone far," I said, diving under to have a look. I was forgetting I wasn't in a swimming pool. My eyes were really stinging when I came up.

"I shouldn't have done that," I said, rubbing them.

"Don't rub them, Ollie, you'll only make it worse. I'm just going back up to the others. I think Charlie's got a spare scrunchie."

She went rushing off and I stood there blinking to try and get the salt out of my eyes. If only I had some ordinary cold water and then I could wash my face. I was on the point of going back to Mom for a towel when a horrible sight met my eyes.

At the back of the beach was an expanse of huge rocks, and beyond that was the road. There were walkways every so often between the rocks so that people could get from the road to the beach. From where I was in the water it was practically impossible to see anything beyond the beach. I could make out Mom and the others, but only because of our big blue and white beach umbrella. The people coming down the walkways looked like the tiniest dots. But my stomach flipped over at the sight of two dots that were slightly larger than the rest. A pink one and a red one. Oh God!

They'd obviously decided to come anyway. And they'd only got to turn right at the bottom of that walkway and they'd be heading straight for our spot. The game would be up. My sins would catch up with me. Oh, what a mess! What a totally stupid mess!

But then a small miracle happened because they turned left. Maybe I wouldn't be discovered after all. As long as we didn't meet up in the ocean, I reckoned we could avoid them on the beach. I couldn't imagine Mrs. Cotteril or Daisy's mom wanting to go into the cold water, and I bet Daisy wouldn't go in on her own. I'd just have to make sure nobody went on any long walks in their direction. The pink and red dots with the two smaller dots beside them were still walking along purposefully. The more they kept going, the better I felt.

Frankie was on her way back to the ocean, her hair all scrunched up again. Just as she splashed her way up to me, the pink and red dots came to a standstill. Panic over. Frankie and I surfed for another few minutes, but I couldn't relax because I had to keep checking that the coast was clear.

"What are you staring at, Ollie?"

"The sky . . . up there. I was just thinking it's looking a bit overcast."

She looked at me as though I was out of my mind. "Ollie, it's bright blue!"

I was just wondering what to say to that, when she forgot all about the sky because her hair was flying loose.

"Oh no! Not again! I don't believe it! That's the second scrunchie I've lost. Charlie'll kill me.

Sorry, Ollie, I think I'll go and sunbathe for a bit."

"Yeah, OK. I'll go for a walk. See you soon."

I guessed Mom and Peter would be wondering what on earth had happened to Sam and Daisy. I didn't particularly want to be around for that conversation. I walked along at the edge of the water for ages until I was way past the spot where Sam and the others were, then I went straight up the beach towards the road and jogged up one of the little walkways. Once on the road, I turned to go in the other direction and kept going until I figured I was directly above Sam and the others.

I stepped gingerly on the rocks, keeping low and listening hard. Eventually I heard Daisy's mom talking. I stopped and crouched in a little dip in the rocks, a big boulder hiding me from anyone on the beach.

" . . . absolute bliss. I'm so glad we decided to

come anyway. Shopping with the children would have been a bit of a nightmare."

They both chuckled. Then the next voice I heard was Sam's, only he sounded much louder. It took me a moment to work out that this was because he and Daisy must have been actually sitting on the rocks, only a couple of yards away from my boulder. They were to one side of me, and their moms were on the beach to the other side. So though I could hear both pairs talking, they couldn't hear each other.

"Oh, come *on*, Daisy," Sam was saying. "*Pleeeease* come into the ocean with me. This is so boring. I'd bet you'd go in if Ollie wanted you to."

"Yes, I would. But he isn't here, is he?"

"Well, I'm not being boring just because Frankie's not here. Come on, Daisy. We can have one raft each. You don't get cold or wet on a raft." I winced. Then I winced even more with his next words. "I wonder if she's missing me.

I bet she's really fed up, being ill."

"Look, I'm trying to read this magazine, Sam. Can you be quiet, please?"

I'd heard enough and was about to go back to Frankie and the others when Mrs. Cotteril's words stopped me.

"Well, would you believe it!"

My heart beat faster.

"Look over there, Letitia! Unless my eyes are deceiving me, that is Sue and Peter Cranshaw!"

My blood ran cold.

"My goodness, you're right. That's odd. Perhaps they decided the children were well enough after all."

"You *are* sure you heard Sue right, Letitia?"

"Well . . . I'm beginning to wonder now. As I said, the line was terrible."

"Look! The children are there! Well, bless me! They're playing away without a care in the world."

"No, wait a minute. There are only three of them."

My heart was banging against my ribs by this time. Their voices were getting louder, and I was afraid Sam and Daisy would hear them.

"It's Ollie who's missing. I wonder if Sue meant it was Ollie not Rory who was unwell. Maybe they decided he was old enough to be left alone for a little while."

"Unless . . ." There was a long pause. "No, it can't be . . ."

"What?'

"You don't think they were trying to get out of having Daisy and Sam with them?"

"No, no, no. I don't know Sue all that well, but I'm quite certain there's nothing artful about her. Let's pop over and have a word, shall we?" She lowered her voice and I only just caught what she said next. "Better not tell Daisy and Sam at this stage." Then she called out, "We're just stretching our legs, you two. Back in a sec."

I groaned. So this was it. The game was up.

13. SHOCK WAVES

Every muscle in my body tightened up. I didn't wait another second, just scrambled back up the rocks, ignoring the pain in the soles of my feet, ran for ages along the road, then went down a walkway on the other side of Mom and the others.

"Been running, Ollie? You're puffing," said Mom.

"I've just come from over there," I said, pointing in the opposite direction to where Sam and Daisy were. "It's really amazing. There are rock pools and everything. You wanna move places?"

"You're joking, Ollie. This is perfect," said Mom in a lazy voice because she was half asleep in the sun.

"You haven't said anything about our castle," called Charlie. "Look! Don't you think it's awesome? We just need to fill up the moat now."

I glanced along the beach. They were about a minute away. There was nothing I could do. I suddenly understood what it meant when people talked about "burying your head in the sand." I wished I could've buried my whole body.

"Oh, here they are at last," said Frankie, sitting up. "We thought you weren't coming!" she called out. "Can you pass me my sun block, Ollie? It's in that bag."

"I'm going down to the water."

"Just pass Frankie her sun block, Ollie," said Mom.

"Hello," said Peter to Mrs. Cotteril and her

sister. "Have you left your stuff in the car? Do you want a hand?"

Mom must have suddenly sensed that something was wrong.

"Where are Sam and Daisy, Pammy? Is everything all right?"

"I think that should be *our* question," said Sam's mom, a bit snappily.

I was about to creep off when Frankie asked me to pass her sunglasses. I started rummaging in the bag that she was pointing at.

"Sorry?" said Mom, shielding her eyes from the sun and looking bewildered.

"I thought two of the children weren't well," went on Mrs. Cotteril.

"Sorry?" said Mom again, sounding puzzled.

"The last we heard, Frankie and Rory were unwell so this beach trip was off."

"I don't understand. Who did you hear that from?"

"From you!"

"I'm afraid I'm really not following this."

"Just tell us what on earth you're talking about," said Peter, sounding a bit tense. I shot him a quick look. We all did. It was very rare for Peter to get riled by anything or anyone.

"At seven o'clock this morning we received a phone call from you, Sue, to say that Frankie and Rory were unwell so you were going to have to cancel today's arrangements."

"But I . . . I . . ."

"Hold on a minute."

That was Peter. He was scanning our faces. Mine, Frankie's, Charlie's and Rory's. He settled on mine.

"Do you know anything about this, Ollie?"

I had a split second to decide whether or not to come clean. And in that split second I heard Sam's smarmy voice in my mind . . . *I'm going to get her to kiss me.*

"No. Don't know what you're talking about."

I managed to hold Peter's gaze until he moved on to Frankie. "What about you?"

She shook her head and I saw suspicion in Peter's eyes.

He thinks it's her.

"Charlie? Rory? Anything to say before we pack up and go straight home?"

I'd never heard Peter sounding so angry before. Inside my head an argument raged.

Just own up.

I'll only get punished.

You deserve it.

But I might be able to get away with it.

The longer it goes on, the worse it'll get.

It can't be worse than having to put up with Sam and Daisy.

So you're prepared to ruin the rest of the holiday for everyone?

I can't own up now. Not in front of them all.

I'll do it as soon as I'm on my own with Mom or Peter.

Promise?

Promise.

"Well, Charlie?" Peter repeated.

"What exactly are you saying, Dad?" asked Charlie, standing up to her father in her usual way.

"I'm saying that Daisy's mom received a phone call this morning at seven o'clock and it was not made by Sue or me. So which one of you four is going to own up?"

"I didn't get up till a quarter to eight, so it wasn't me," said Charlie. "What time did you get up, Rory?"

Everyone knew that Rory was always first up. "I don't know. I didn't even look at my watch, but Ollie wasn't in bed when I woke up."

All eyes were back on me.

"Look, I've told you, it wasn't me . . ."

Mom suddenly took charge of the situation.

"Pammy, all I can do is to apologize profusely."

"Don't worry, my dear. We're just along there. You can see our mauve beach umbrella, can't you? It's the tall one."

"Yes . . . thank you. Just give us a few minutes."

There was a silence when they'd gone. Then Peter said, "Right, I'm going to give you all one more chance to own up and if no one does, we go home. Simple as that." There was another silence. "And I mean *home*, not holiday house."

He delivered this last stab in a low voice that made goosebumps come up on my arms even though the sun was shining. I glanced at Frankie. A tear was running down her face.

"I did it," she said softly.

Charlie, Rory, Mom, Peter and I all stared at her, wide-eyed. I couldn't bear it any longer. Frankie must have been so desperate not to end the holiday she was prepared to take the blame for something that she hadn't even done.

"No, *I* did it," I said. I looked Peter straight in the eye. "I know I've done a terrible thing, but I just couldn't stomach the thought of those two being with us for yet another day. That's all. Sorry. You can punish me, Peter, but please don't make us all go home."

Peter and Mom looked at each other, then Mom spoke to Charlie and Rory. "Why don't you two go ahead and fill up your moat with water?"

Without a word they grabbed their buckets and went off. I was about to be blasted into oblivion. And yet when I looked back on this moment much later, all I could remember was the way Charlie and Rory had looked so odd, going down to the water, their two thin tense bodies walking close together to try and ward off the awful atmosphere.

"I trust you're not just protecting Frankie, Oliver," said Peter.

I think that was the first time he'd ever called me Oliver. It was like a double shock because I suddenly realized that he really didn't know which one of us had done it. Frankie stayed silent. I shook my head and looked down. When I looked back up again, he was peering into Frankie's face, as though to sniff out any lies that might be lurking inside her head.

There were lots of tears on her face, but she didn't make a sound when she was crying. I think I liked her more in that moment than I'd ever liked her before. She could have easily thrown a big fit and screamed at her dad that it wasn't her, but she didn't say a word.

I had to put her out of her agony.

"I got up really early and went outside with your cell phone, Mom. I took it behind the hedge on the other side of the road and I imitated your voice and told Daisy's mom it was all off because of Frankie and Rory being ill."

"But why, Oliver?" said Mom in a quiet voice. "I mean, it's a bit drastic, isn't it? Why didn't you just tell me and Peter that you'd be happier if we didn't have Sam and Daisy for the day?"

"Because you'd think I was stupid and you'd tell the others and then Rory would start on me. And anyway, you wouldn't have been able to cancel it at such short notice."

"Well, that's probably true, but at least we could have made sure we didn't make any further arrangements. We're all on this holiday together, Oliver. Everyone has a right to be happy."

"Yeah, but I would have been outvoted. I knew I was the only one who didn't want them around."

"You weren't, actually."

Frankie had finally spoken. I couldn't believe my ears. I wanted to know what she meant, but Rory was racing back from the water, shouting something and waving his arms frantically.

We strained to hear.

"Quick. Sam's fallen off his raft!"

I shot up and set off full speed.

"Oliver! Come back here!" I heard Peter's angry voice. "You're not getting off that lightly."

"For goodness' sake. He's only fallen off a raft," shouted Mom irritably.

But I had recognized the panic in Rory's voice.

"Sam can't swim!" I heard Frankie tell them, then I was too far away to hear another word.

14. THE KISS

I ran and ran, the wind drumming in my ears, the roar of the ocean making my legs go faster and faster. As I got nearer I could see the raft, but no Sam.

Charlie was standing by the edge, ready to direct me.

"Over there!" she screamed, pointing to the raft.

"Tell Mom to call for an ambulance or something," I called over my shoulder as I kicked my way as far as I could into the water, then plunged into the fastest front crawl I could manage, swimming hard till I knew I must be out of my depth. I was getting nearer and nearer to the raft, yet Sam was nowhere to be seen. I dove under, keeping my eyes open. The water stung my already sore eyes but I didn't care. Sam was under the raft. His face looked strange. I grabbed hold of him under the arms and pushed him up to the surface, then realized that his weight was making us both go under. I had to get him on the raft.

"Sam!" I said breathlessly. "Can you hear me?"

His eyes were closed and his head was lolling. I was terrified. What if . . . I couldn't bear it if . . .

He was too heavy to put on the raft. I knew then that I hadn't time to do anything other than struggle to the shore as best I could. I'd practiced lifesaving lots of times in school swimming lessons, but this wasn't the same as trying it out on a partner who floated obediently on the surface, hanging lightly on to you, while you swam easily to the side. I used all my strength to try to keep Sam's head above water as I struggled along.

You could hardly call it swimming, what I did. I was kicking my legs violently and shoving the water with my shoulders and head. I swallowed loads of water along the way and thought I was going to be sick. I could hear lots of people having fun swimming and splashing near by, but they didn't notice me in my little terrifying world, and I couldn't shout for help because I needed all my energy to stop Sam from going under. I felt sick and I thought my arms were going to drop off.

"Please don't die, Sam," I spluttered, though I knew he couldn't hear me. "You can kiss Frankie as much as you want. Just please don't die."

And suddenly my feet were touching the

bottom and I could stand — except that I couldn't because my knees were crumbling. Someone was yelling and running towards me. It was Peter.

"Hang in there, Ollie. You've done great."

He was really panting as I dropped Sam into his arms. Another man was instantly at our side. Between them they carried Sam on to the shore.

"I think he's going to need mouth to mouth," the man said to Peter. "I'm not too sure . . ."

"Um . . . neither am I. You're supposed to clear the airways first, aren't you?" said Peter. I saw that he was shaking.

"I'll do it," I said, kneeling over Sam and taking charge.

This bit, I could remember well. Peter got out of the way quickly. I put two fingers under Sam's chin and tipped his head back.

Right, what's next? Check breathing. Look, listen, feel. Count to ten. Not breathing. OK, block nose . . . mouth to mouth. Five breaths. Keep calm, Ollie.

A small crowd was gathering. I was vaguely aware of toes clenching the sand near Sam's head. Nothing else.

Take pulse at Adam's apple. Yes! A pulse! But he was still unconscious. *What now? Keep doing it. Twenty breaths, check pulse, twenty breaths, take pulse . . . until help arrives.*

"You're doing well, Ollie," said Peter, his voice still shaking.

Sam's mom had arrived on the scene. I could hear her wailing.

"I had no idea he'd gone into the ocean."

Mom and Daisy's mom were trying to calm her, but they didn't sound calm themselves.

"Don't worry, Pammy. He'll be all right."

There were other voices too, but they were a blur. My head was swimming. I thought I couldn't last much longer. After every breath

I gave Sam, I said *Please live* inside my head.

"The ambulance is on its way."

The pulse was still there. Was it my imagination or was it weaker? If anything happened to Sam, it would be my fault. I'd never be able to bear it. Nothing mattered any more, except getting my friend back. *Surely someone will be here in a minute.*

And just at that very moment Sam threw up a load of sea water, then his chest shuddered. I sat back in a crouched position as he rolled over on to his side and opened his eyes.

"Oh Sam!" cried his mother, dropping on to her knees beside him.

As the ambulance men arrived with the stretcher, I stood up shakily.

"Someone's done a great job here," said one of the men.

"It was my brother," said Rory. "His name's Ollie."

Rory had tears in his eyes and was really shouting at the men as though they were deaf.

"Well, that's one amazing brother you've got there, son," said the ambulance man as he helped the other man roll Sam on to the stretcher.

"He's *my* brother too!" came another voice. It was Frankie. She was suddenly beside me giving me an enormous hug. I couldn't hug her back because I still felt too weak.

"And mine!" Charlie called.

"Sounds like you've got a good bunch of brothers and sisters!" said the ambulance man to me.

Sam was trying to sit up. He looked totally confused and his eyes didn't seem to be focusing properly.

"All right, son, what's your name?"

"Sam," he whispered.

"I'm his mother," said Mrs. Cotteril.

"We'll get Sam to hospital and check him over," said the first ambulance man. "Don't you worry now, my dear . . ." Then the man turned to me. "What exactly happened, Ollie?"

"He saved Sam's life," said Mrs. Cotteril, bursting into tears as we all set off.

Peter's arm was around my shoulder and we both had shaky legs as we walked a few paces behind the stretcher. Mom was beside me on the other side.

"I'm so proud of you," she whispered.

The three girls were walking behind with Daisy's mom but Rory was walking beside Sam, telling him all that had happened in a very loud slow voice, as though the ocean might have addled Sam's brain.

"Ollie!" he suddenly called back to me. "Sam wants you."

I broke free from Peter and caught up with the stretcher. Sam looked up at me. I was glad to see his eyes were back to normal. In fact his whole face was back to normal, except he looked funny without his glasses.

"Thanks for saving my life, Ollie."

I didn't know what to say. I couldn't really say, "Oh, that's OK," as though I'd lent him fifty cents or something.

"Ollie . . ."

He was beckoning me to bend down, so I did, rather awkwardly as I kept walking.

"I knew I'd get to kiss *someone* today. I just never guessed it'd be you!"

An hour before I would have happily throttled him for a remark like that. But now, for some unknown reason, I didn't care. I really didn't care.

15. FRIENDS

It was six o'clock in the evening and Frankie and I were sitting side by side on a wall in the yard. All the others were inside the house setting up the score sheet for another tournament.

"Sorry about today," I said without looking at her.

"You've already said sorry, Ollie. You don't need to keep saying it."

"I know I've apologized to Mom and Peter, but I haven't apologized to you. And I haven't said thanks either."

"What for?"

"Taking the blame so we wouldn't have to go home early."

"It was the only way I could thing of getting you to own up."

"What do you mean?"

"Well, I know my dad. And today it was pretty obvious that unless one of us owned up, we were in for some kind of awful punishment. I knew you were too nice to let me take the blame . . ."

She smiled at me. It was one of those really genuine smiles that I'd seen her giving Sam. This time yesterday, I was a stupid lovesick teenager and that smile would have sent me up to forty-seventh heaven. But today everything was different. It was impossible to explain — even to myself — what had changed. It was when I was struggling through the water desperately trying to save Sam, that I'd suddenly realized friendship was the most important thing. The only thing that counted. All I wanted now was to have Frankie as my best friend. I knew it would take time, though.

She was biting her lip, watching me biting *my* lip. There was so much I wanted to talk to her about, but I didn't want to say anything that would make her think I was a complete dork.

"When we were on the beach, you told Mom and Peter that I wasn't the only one who didn't want Sam and Daisy to join us today."

"Yeah. That was true."

"Why?"

"You'll think I'm horrible."

"I won't. Honest."

She looked down and mumbled, "I thought you had a thing for Daisy and I didn't want my brother going out with someone as uncool as her."

"Oh . . . er . . . yeah . . ." She'd really surprised me. "Sorry about that," I said, feeling embarrassed about the way the conversation was going.

"Please tell me you don't like her like that."

"No, I don't. You see, I thought you liked Sam, and — "

"Sam? You've got to be joking! What ever made you think that?"

I suddenly felt stupid. "Well, you seemed to be kind of talking to him and stuff . . ."

"Talking to him? Since when did talking to someone mean you loved them? I was just being friendly."

Then I really felt stupid. "Well, he likes you," I mumbled.

"Yeah, I worked that one out. That was the other reason I didn't want those two around for another day. It was easy being friendly for one afternoon, but when Daisy wanted them both to join us *again* I felt suicidal. And there's another thing . . ."

"What?"

"You'll think I'm stupid."

For the second time I assured her I wouldn't.

"Well, you see those first few days on the beach were so fantastic, and then everything seemed to go wrong. You didn't seem to like me much any more . . ."

"Yeah, I did. It's just that Rory – well, Rory gets things wrong a lot . . . and he might have thought I had a crush on you, or something totally stupid like that. So I didn't want to seem too . . . you know . . . friendly."

She looked at me carefully and I knew I was going red, but there was nothing I could do about it.

"I wish I'd known that. You see, I'd been so happy to find that I got on absolutely perfectly with my brother, and I just wanted those first few days to go on for ever. Then I heard you telling Rory that if you were dreaming about me, it must have been a nightmare, and I thought you didn't like me after all."

I felt terrible when she said that. "It was just to shut Rory up. Honest."

"I believe you now. The trouble is, once we're all back home again, I won't get to see you very much, but you can see Sam whenever you like. And then there was Daisy. It was jealousy, I suppose. I didn't want those two around because I wanted you all to myself. Simple as that."

Suddenly everything was clear. Frankie didn't have feelings for me *or* Sam, and she'd never had. She just liked me as a brother and wanted me to like her as a sister. I felt really happy all of a sudden. Maybe one day she'd even want me as her best friend.

"Come on!" Mom called out to us. "We're

about to start the tournament. You two are partners."

"And guess what?" said Rory as we went in to join the others.

"What?"

"Peter's going to ask Charlie's mom if Charlie can come over more often from now on."

Frankie and I looked at each other and slowly broke into big smiles. It was such an obvious solution.

"What are you two grinning about?" asked Rory.

"You," I told him. "We're thinking what a clever thing you've just said."

Rory looked at us suspiciously.

"No, really," said Frankie. "It's the best thing that's happened this whole holiday. Apart from Ollie saving the life of his second best friend in the world," she added.

"Second best? So who's his *best* friend then?"

asked Rory, looking as puzzled as I felt.

"Me, of course," she told him. Then she turned to me and smiled.

So when Rory gave me yet another of his big slow-motion winks, it didn't tick me off one little bit. In fact I just cracked up laughing! And so did Frankie.

What happens next in the step-chain?
Meet Lissie in

SHE'S NO ANGEL

1. THE BOMBSHELL

"Hey ya'll!" said Leanne, chucking her school bag on her desk, which was just across the aisle from mine.

Her three good friends gathered around immediately.

"What have you been up to this weekend, Leanne? You've got that look on your face again!"

Leanne giggled.

I dread this time, first thing Monday morning, when you talk about what you've been doing on the weekend. Today I'd happened to come in at exactly the same time as Leanne, so all the attention would be on her. She's the sort of leader of the group, whereas I'm only on the edge because I'm not as good at making friends. Everyone always gathers around Leanne, and right now she was looking as though she was about to report something really interesting. With any luck I might escape the Monday morning interrogation.

"I went to New York City!" She announced, looking around proudly.

Gasps went up.

"How come you never told us on Friday?" asked Donna.

Leanne suddenly let out her breath and pulled a face as she spoke slowly. "Because it was nothing great. It was my brother's graduation ceremony, and though Mom and Dad were in seventh heaven for the entire weekend, I was actually so bored I counted the bricks in the wall behind the stage!"

Everyone laughed. Leanne always makes people want to talk to her and laugh with her. I wish I could do that. Even when she's had a boring weekend, she's still swinging along happily.

"I went to my cousin's birthday party on Saturday night and it was so cool!" said Donna.

"You lucky thing!" said Leanne, pouting and pretending she was jealous.

"I danced for three solid hours! The music was great!"

"Yeah, and Donna and I went shopping in that new mall," said Jo. "Mom was in a really good mood. She gave me an advance on my allowance and I bought those black pants I wanted *and* that pink top!"

I pretended to be looking in my school bag, and started silently chanting my usual prayer for every other Monday morning: *Please don't ask me what I've been doing.* I can't bear it when they all look at me as though they feel sorry for me, so recently I've started pretending I've had a great time at my mom's. I'm not sure they're convinced though, and that makes it even worse. They probably talk about me afterwards behind my back.

"What did you do, Gemma?"

I breathed out. I was off the hook again.

"My aunt and uncle came for the weekend."

"Cool! The uncle who works at Channel 4?"

"Yeah. He told us some great stories."

I couldn't scrabble around in my bag for ever and as I glanced up I saw Leanne looking at me. Uh-oh! Here we go.

"What did *you* do, Lissie?"

I frowned at my nails then began to gnaw at one of them. I was getting very good at appearing unconcerned when inside I was completely churned up.

"Oh, nothing much . . ."

"Was it your weekend to go to your mom's?"

"Yeah."

There was a pause and I could feel everyone's eyes on me. They were waiting for me to say something else. But how could I tell them what had really happened?

We went to Toby and Petronella's school fair on Saturday afternoon, where they both got to do and buy just about everything they wanted, and when they didn't win the games, they sulked. On Sunday morning I practiced my cello which wasn't easy, because my half-sister was deliberately playing her music loudly in her bedroom.

I didn't say anything.

"What did you do on Saturday? Anything good?"

This was it. Either I had to tell the truth and admit that I'd had a totally terrible time because I couldn't stand my eight-year-old half-sister and my five-year-old half-brother, or I had to tell the usual lie and pretend that I'd had a great time. But I felt so pathetic admitting that I'd had another miserable weekend. It made me look stupid for not doing something about it. And I knew I *was* stupid. It was just so much easier to suffer in silence. After all, it was only two little days out of every fourteen – or even sometimes only one. And they *were* my half-sister and -brother.

"Nothing much . . ." I quickly changed the subject. "Has anyone got any nail polish remover on them?"

I didn't miss the look that passed between Donna and Leanne. I bet they were thinking, *Imagine putting up with spending every other weekend with two children you can't stand. How sad is that?*

It was a quarter past six when Dad got home.

Gemma's mom had just dropped me back from music club, as she did every Monday.

"Hi, Liss," Dad said to me, as he started opening the mail. "How was school?"

"Fine."

I was sure he wasn't concentrating on me at all.

"We had choir practice at lunchtime."

"Uh-huh."

He screwed up the contents of the envelope, made a ball out of it and aimed it at the bin, before opening the next envelope.

"And I got C minus for that biology homework that you helped me with. So thanks very much, Dad."

"Uh-huh."

He was scanning through a phone bill, a frown on his face.

"We had some visitors at school this afternoon."

"Uh-huh."

Right, Dad, let's see if you're really listening.

"Yeah. Some gorillas. They just strolled in and started taking over from the teachers."

"Uh-huh."

"One of them was called Goliath, and I hope you don't mind but I liked him so much that I've signed the adoption papers and he's up in my bedroom watching TV with a banana and a bag of cheese and onion chips."

Dad stopped reading and gave me a vague sort of smile. "That's great," he said. "Sorry – who did you say was upstairs?"

"You weren't listening to a single word I said, Dad."

"Yes I was!" he protested. "I just didn't hear who you said was in your room."

"Goliath the gorilla!" I informed him, with a withering look, to show him just how hopeless he was.

He looked a bit embarrassed then. "Sorry,

Liss. Has my black shirt come out of the wash?"

"I think so. Why? Are you going out?"

"Yes, in about an hour. I'm going to . . ."

He broke off and sat down at the table. Suddenly I knew that he was about to say something important. Half a dozen possibilities flashed through my mind. Maybe he and Pauline had had a big argument and Dad had found himself a new girlfriend. That would be terrible because I really like Pauline. Dad's only been going out with her for about a month, but he seems so happy. I'd hate it if they broke up. She isn't the first girlfriend Dad's had since he and Mom split up all those years ago, but even though I've only met her a few times I've got a feeling she's something special, and that Dad thinks so too.

Maybe he's taking her out for dinner and he's going to propose to her. That would be great! I'd get to be a bridesmaid. Then she could come and live in this house and I'd feel like I was in a proper family again. OK, I knew I was only building castles in the air, because you don't usually get married when you've only known someone a month.

Dad was looking at me carefully. "The thing is, Liss . . . Pauline and I . . ." My heart hammered, " . . . are going away together. Someone at work has got a place in Portugal, and we're going to rent it. So this evening we're meeting this guy and his wife to sort out the details."

It was weird. It was like a bombshell without an explosion. I couldn't work out what the big deal was. It was great that Dad and Pauline had decided to have a holiday together. Maybe that would make them want to live together all the time. So why was my heart still banging away?

With Dad's next words I suddenly knew.

"You'll be staying at Mom's, Liss."

He was giving me one of those encouraging

smiles that you give little kids when you're telling them how great it is at the dentist's.

I didn't want him to feel guilty about going away with Pauline, because Dad hardly ever does anything except work, so I tried to sound unfazed.

"How long for?"

Please let it only be a week.

"Two weeks."

My heart stopped hammering and plummeted to my toes.

Collect the links in the step-chain . . .

1. To see her dad Sarah has to stay with the woman who wrecked her family. Will she do it? Find out in *One Mom Too Many!*

3. Lissie's half-sister is a spoiled brat, but her mom thinks she's adorable. Can Lissie make her see what's really going on? Find out in *She's No Angel*

4. Becca's mom describes her boyfriend's daughter as perfect in every way. Can Becca bear to meet her? Find out in *Too Good To Be True*

5. Ed's stepsisters are getting seriously on his nerves. Should he go and live with his mom? Find out in *Get Me Out Of Here*

6. Hannah and Rachel are stepsisters. They're also best friends. What will happen to them if their parents split up? Find out in *Parents Behaving Badly*